Saving Grace

Sandy Thrush

Just-For-Fun Publishing
Kentwood, Michigan
~2008~

SAVING GRACE © 2007 by Sandy Thrush

All rights reserved. No portion of this book may be reproduced, stored in a retrieval system, or transmitted in any form or by any means – electronic, mechanical, photocopy, recording, or other – except for brief quotations in printed reviews, without the prior permission of the publisher.

Published by Just-For-Fun Publishing, PO Box 888162, Kentwood, MI 49588-8162.

Print production by: Central Plains Book~A Division of Sun Graphic, Arkansas City, KS
Cover production by: Sadie Cross, BRIOprint, LLC, Minneapolis, MN

Just-For-Fun Publishing books may be purchased in bulk for educational, business, fundraising, or sales promotional use. For information, please email Just4FunPublishing@gmail.com or visit our web site at www.justforfunpublishing.com.

Scripture quotations used in this book are from *The Holy Bible*, The Bible in Basic English, World English Bible, King James Authorized Version, The Webster Bible Translation, and the NIV Translation from CrossDaily.com online Bible Search.

Words from songs used by permission:
Keep Holding On
Words & music by David Elchler & Kevin Shorey
Fresh Rain Productions,
A division of Lowell Lundstrom Ministries.
Peace Be Still
Writer Credits: Jeff Nelson / Al Denson
© 1989 HeartService Music (admin. By Music Services)/Paragon Music (admin. By Brentwood-Benson Music Publishing, Inc.)
All Rights Reserved. ASCAP
I Can Begin Again
Writer Credits: Dave Clark / Larnelle Harris
© 1989 First Row Music/John T. Benson Publishing Co. Inc/Bridge Building
I Can Not Hide From You
Writer Credits: Tony Wood / Scott Krippayne / Steven Rimmon Siler © New Spring Publishing, Inc./Word Music, LLC
©2003 Silerland Music(Admin. By Word Music, LLC/All Rights Reserved

Publisher's Note: This "story" is a work of fiction. Names, characters, places, are products of the author's imagination or are used fictitiously. Some of the incidences are loosely drawn from real life incidents of the author and other resources.

ISBN 978-0-9821371-0-9

INTRODUCTION

The Author of *"Saving Grace"* calls her book fiction. Names, characters, and places changed, incidents and circumstances, no doubt, modified to facilitate the author's intent to protect and preserve the varied personalities instrumental in shaping not only her own personal history, but that of all her resources. Yet, I have seen similar lessons learned and experiences recorded, carved out on the fabric of her soul and the souls of numerous others. This book is not a fantasy of some far off distant place in the over-active imagination of her mind, but a true testimony of hell pushed back, and the restoration of a soul called forth.

Her purpose for telling this story is to share it with those who so desperately need to hear that there is hope, and that a personal relationship with Jesus Christ *is that Hope!*

Her prayer and ours is that the Holy Spirit will work through the telling of this story, so all who read it might come to know and experience personally God's *"saving grace"*, and the truth of His Word. May we all be moved beyond the confines of guilt, fear and anger, rejecting all the failing mechanisms of self-preservation to become whole and complete in the all-knowing and loving arms of our dearest Friend and Savior, Jesus Christ.

Thank you Sandy and thank you Jesus for such a willing and ready vessel, a special gift, molded by the Master's hand.

Ken & BK Zimmer
07/13/06

Note from the Author

I think, for a long as I can remember, I have wanted to be a writer. Stories and books have always been a big part of my life. But wanting to write and writing are two different things. I did not think that I would ever really be able to write a story that would capture a reader's heart and soul, one that would pull at their very deepest emotions, and lift them to heights of joy, praise, peace, worship and hope. "Saving Grace" is my endeavor to do just that.

"Saving Grace" is being marketed as a work of fiction. Names, characters, and places have been changed; incidents and circumstances modified to facilitate my intent to protect and preserve the varied personalities instrumental in shaping not only my own personal history, but also that of all my resources. So, while this book is a work of fiction, in truth, it is the true story of a real person. Cousin May, your best friend, Amy, a lost and hurting co-worker, or the neighbor down the street. Most who read this will see someone they know in the character, Grace. The really true theme that runs like a golden thread throughout this story is the restoring power of a loving God, whose mercy and grace are there for all who are hurting and oppressed. He is there. We are not alone in our struggles, and most important, He is the God of new beginnings.

Even as this book is going to press, I know I did not do this on my own. I know this because of the flow of the writing of it. The Holy Spirit, Himself, was my guide. Without Him, this book would not be. But I also have so many others to thank for all their help and encouragement.

BK and Ken, who said this story NEEDED to be told, so the hurting and oppressed could see that Jesus Christ is THE HOPE they are looking for.

Cyndi Harper-Deiters, my sister-in-Christ, my mentor, my friend, who constantly lifted me up and told me that this story was a beacon of hope for the hurting, and willingly shared her knowledge of the writing process.

Esther Ayotte, who spent hours editing and fine-tuning my book in preparation for publication, thank you, thank you, thank you!

I cannot list every person who was instrumental in some way in this long process, but my heart thanks all of you. My prayer is truly that all who read this will see the truth – that a personal relationship with Jesus Christ is the HOPE we have, that we can stand on, when all around us is sinking sand. He's right there, waiting to lift us up, we just have to reach out to Him.

God Bless

Sandy

~ Prologue ~

Grace peeked past the curtain to look out at the auditorium. It was filling up fast. Seemed like it always did. The sea of faces blurred slightly as the familiar feeling of last minute jitters washed over her like a raging flood.
Dear heavenly Father, please help me!
Grace looked at her watch: thirty-five more minutes. She took a deep breath and closed her eyes. Tonight's meeting was especially meaningful to her. Thirteen years ago today she had inadvertently started on a long journey. A soft sad smile touched her face like gentle caressing fingers on the edge of her mind. Her memories flowed back in time to that Friday in June 1989. That was the day when her tortured existence had finally pushed her to drastic measures, and the journey had begun that changed her life forever. . . .

Chapter 1

Grace slowly walked across the smooth mosaic tile floor of the formal dining room toward the kitchen. She turned in the doorway to look back at the rich mahogany dining room set for the last time. The soothingly elegant table easily sat twelve people in the rich orchid cushioned high back chairs. The tall buffet and hutch held a set of china dishes in a soft pastel orchid pattern, with matching crystal glassware also etched with orchids. This room alone would have made any woman happy. So why had it not made her happy? *For God's sake, tell yourself the truth, Grace. Just this last time, tell your self the truth. It's your secret, the untold violations that have stripped you of your joy, your reason for living.* Grace shook her head, trying to stop her own train of thought.

The morning sun shone through the delicate lace curtains casting a pleasing design on the table as her thoughts turned to the high hopes and dreams that had prompted her choice of the ornate furniture and dishes. What had happened to those hopes and dreams? It seemed like they belonged to another person in a different time and place. *Well, it doesn't matter now*, she thought, and turned hopelessly back into the kitchen.

Her deep blue eyes took in the warm cozy kitchen. How she had loved designing the unique layout. Their builder had almost had a fit when she insisted on both hardwood plank and slate for the flooring. But, it had been worth the fight. The effect was breathtaking against the hardwood and glass cupboards. Her vision blurred as her eyes filled with tears remembering the many meals she had prepared, trying to please Justin. For some reason nothing was ever done to his liking. A bitter taste rose in her throat, and she actually laughed, an almost hysterical laugh. Yah, nothing was to his liking, *unless* it happened to be in the master suite, his private torture chamber.

She had tried to believe that her busy schedule at "You Asked For It Designs, Inc." had prompted his suggestion of hiring a housekeeper. At the time she thought it meant he was concerned for her. It wasn't long, though, until she realized hiring a housekeeper was part of his obsession with success and impressing his circle of colleagues. Fortunately, she had liked Mrs. Feldman the first time she met her. Pat was a kind gentle widow whose sweet nature and temperament had drawn Grace to her like bees to flowers. Grace had even grown accustom to her reading the Bible and always talking to her about Jesus. There had been something so comfortable and familiar about her nature. Their friendship had grown over the years. The years?

Grace walked over to the breakfast bar where she had set a full glass of water with two bottles of pills. Pulling out one of the hardwood stools, she sat down on the edge of the seat. How many years had it been? She and Justin had been married for nine years now, nine long tormenting years. No, that was not entirely true. They had not all been a horrifying nightmare. The first two and half years had been like a fantasy, except for an occasional incident. She had almost convinced herself they had not really happened.

When they moved into what she

2

thought was their dream house over their second anniversary, she had high hopes that *the incidents* would stop completely. She had really been proud of Justin when he became a junior partner in the law firm after only eighteen months. It meant late nights and long weekends away from home for him. When he insisted on hiring a housekeeper, she immersed herself in her job and managing their home with Pat's help. Pat had been with them for almost six years. It was ironic, really, because now she knew that Justin would have fired Pat years ago if he had known what a comfort she had become to Grace.

Actually, Pat was the reason she had waited as long as she had. Knowing how much Pat was going to be hurt by what she was doing had kept her from following through with her plan. Even so, the memories of the last two days and nights had only made her more determined in her decision; today was the day. Even though the *incidents* only happened on Pat's nights off, their intensity had increased to the point of overwhelming devastation. She could no longer hide it from Pat, but neither could she face the thought of telling her.

She had sent Pat off on an errand shortly after she had come in this morning hoping to spare her some small fraction of pain. Her narrow shoulders slumped in defeat as she stared at the pills she had dumped out on the counter. Though she still had plenty of pills, she had refilled the prescription. Her hands shook as she counted out the pills. *Sixty; surely that should be enough.*

She glanced at the antique clock on the kitchen wall over the white porcelain sink. 10:00 am. *How long will it take,* she wondered? Gripping the large glass of water with her left hand she picked up several pills. Very methodically she took all the pills lying on the counter. With the last of the pills down, she carefully set the glass beside the two empty pill bottles.

Her eyes scanned the note she had written to Justin. Just the thought of him made her tremble involuntarily, an icy cold chill running down her spine like icicles on bare skin. Every muscle in her body ached from the sick tortured treatment she had endured for the last two days and nights. How was she supposed to explain to someone who once protected her, but now was a hideous perpetrator bent on manipulation and found extreme pleasure in inflicting demeaning control over her, that she felt her life was worth less than nothing? Would he even care?

She flinched with pain as she rested her bruised elbows on the smooth cool tile of the counter, and dropped her forehead onto her hands, pinching her eyes tightly shut. Nausea threatened to overwhelm her. She had to keep the pills in her system. *There is no other way, and I am just too tired to keep trying. This has to stop.* Her mind was a tormenting video caught in a loop, playing over and over the two days and nights of unimaginable acts of sexual torture and abuse. Her mind and soul convulsed with sorrow, loss, and grief. Tears forced their way between her swollen eyelids and fingers, falling like raindrops onto the counter. Several spattered her carefully worded note to Justin. Lifting her head and forcing her eyes open, Grace strained to focus on the clock. 10:15 - *how much longer is this going to take?*

Another ten minutes passed before Grace finally stood up, roughly pushing back the stool. It tipped over and crashed to the floor with a resounding thud. She turned, and leaned her small frame back against the wall, and slowly slid to the floor. The room seemed to spin like a top in slow motion. Bright lights in neon colors flashed just off her peripheral vision. A slow booming sound penetrated the dullness of her mind. She wondered in frustration, what it could possibly be. She vaguely entertained the notion of trying to see what and where the sound was coming from, but the heaviness of her arms and legs made standing up impossible. Her breathing was becoming more and more difficult.

I'm dying! I'm really dying! I wonder if there really is a heaven or hell, or is there just. . . nothing? Well, if there is I'm sure I'll be going straight to hell.

Grace closed her eyes, tears still streaming unchecked down her pale, hollow cheeks. Suddenly, as if through a mist, she could see her dad standing off in the distance. He was saying something to her. "What are you saying, Daddy? I can't hear you!" She smiled, trying to lift a drugged heavy hand to wave. *"Daddy, my precious Daddy, where are you? Why did you leave me, just when I needed you so much?"*

Suddenly he was kneeling beside her. *"Grace? What are you doing, honey?"*

Grace slowly lifted her heavy aching head to look into the loving eyes of her father. "Daddy, why did you have to go away? I'm so scared! Everything is so confusing; I don't know how to fix things. My whole life has been one bad dream after another. I'm so alone, and I really don't deserve to live. My life is worthless, and I'm sure Justin doesn't love me, if he ever really did. He hurts me Daddy; he hurts me. I've kept it a secret, Daddy, but I can't any more. I know you always told me, what happens at home stays at home, but I just can't do it any more. You don't know what he makes me do! I know it would be a sin to leave him, but I can't stay either. I'm sorry, Daddy, you must be so disappointed and ashamed of me." Grace tried to focus her eyes on her father's face. It was becoming harder and harder to breath.

Grace could feel her father gently touching her cheek. He smiled. "Grace? Do you remember when I told you why your mother and I named you 'Grace'?" A thick gray fog filled her mind. Hopelessly, she shook her head no.

As the image of her father slowly faded from her vision, his loving, gentle words caressed her into unconsciousness. "Because by grace you have salvation through faith; and that not of yourselves: it is given by God: Not by works, so that no man may take glory to himself. For by His act we were given existence in Christ Jesus to do those good works which God before made ready for us so that we might do them." *

Pat finally got the door opened and came in from shopping for the groceries Grace had sent her to get. She was frustrated that Grace had not come to unlock the door when she had pounded on it with the heel of her shoe. Where could she be?

She found Grace in the kitchen on

*Ephesians 2:8-10 *The Bible in Basic English*

the floor. Her back was to the wall, arms to her sides, palms resting in an upward position. She was unconscious and barely breathing. When the paramedics arrived, Pat was trying to do CPR because Grace had stopped breathing. Only after the paramedics had her breathing again, and in the ambulance on the way to the hospital, did Pat call Justin at his law office to tell him his wife, her darling little employer, had tried to end her life.

Chapter 2

Grace lay in a comatose state for twelve days. She woke slowly from the long heavy drug induced sleep. When she finally focused on her surroundings, she felt sick with the realization of where she was. Memory came back like the pounding of giant waves against hard rocks, bringing on an instant headache. Guilt, shame, remorse, and hopelessness overcame her with a crushing force.

She was not surprised to find Pat, instead of Justin, sitting on the bedside chair holding her hand, which was secured at the wrist with restraints. Pat gently patted her hand, and cried softly. Her head was bowed and her eyes were closed. Grace trembled and turned her head away, forcing her eyes shut. *She's praying for me. Doesn't she know God wrote me off a long time ago? It's not going to help to pray. He's not listening and even if He was, I don't think He cares anymore, if He ever did.*

Tears seeped through her tightly squeezed eyes. In frustration she tried to wipe them off by rubbing her face on the stiff starched pillow since her hands were secured by the restraints. Her movement made Pat's head snap up, and her smoky gray eyes opened wide in surprise.

"Grace? Grace, honey, can you hear me?" The sadness and pain in her voice cut Grace like a knife. Overwhelmed with shame, she kept her face turned away from Pat. It had never occurred to her that she might wake up to discover her plan had failed.

Pat stood now, holding Grace's hand. Her eyes searched Grace's face, which was contorted in pain and sorrow.

"Grace, honey, please talk to me. Please, I want to help you."

Pat's hand was comforting, and Grace squeezed it in an effort to reassure her, still unable to speak.

Pat waited for a moment then gently returned the squeeze. She leaned forward and spoke softly, "Grace, I'm going to go and let the nurse know that you are awake and see if she can get you out of those restraints." And, then she was gone.

Grace turned her head to look where Pat had been standing. Her eyes took in the half empty water bottle, a book and a Bible on the window ledge. There was a cot folded up against the wall with a pillow sitting on it. *I wonder if she's been staying all night with me. What day is it? How long have I been here? Where is Justin? Has he been staying at night with me?* Questions raced through Grace's muddled mind, with no answers. She could hear Pat outside her door, talking to the nurse.

"Why can't you remove the restraints?" Pat's voice was anxious and strained.

"I can't take them off without a doctor's order. When I get back to the desk, I will call Dr. Evans to let her know that Grace has come out of the coma. I'm sure she will want to come in and talk to her right away. She will probably write an order after she sees her. I'll call Dr. Phillips, too. He will want to examine her and will probably want some tests run. But now, I need to check her."

The door opened and a tall thin woman came in followed closely by Pat. Grace entertained the idea of closing her eyes and faking sleep, but Pat

10

looked so hopeful, she could not bring herself to cause her more pain.

After taking her temperature and blood pressure and checking her eyes, the nurse stood silently looking at her. Grace swallowed hard trying to psyche herself up to answer any questions she would be asked. A gentle smile spread across the woman's face, and warmth seemed to flow from her hazel eyes. "Grace, my name is Helen. I'm your nurse, and I will be taking care of you for the rest of the evening. How are you feeling? Do you have any pain or discomfort anywhere?"

Helen paused to let her words register. She was pleased to see the look of panic slowly dissipate from Grace's eyes. Her hand reached out and she gently brushed some stray curls away from Grace's eyes. "Once Dr. Evans comes in to see you, she will probably write an order to remove your restraints, then we can get you in the shower. I'm sure you'll feel a lot better after you've taken a shower."

She waited, searching Grace's face for some sign of comprehension. Finally she sighed, and turned to walk out of the room.

"I feel a little nauseated. I, I think I'm hungry." Grace's words were so soft that Pat was afraid for a minute the nurse had not heard her, but she did. She stopped at the door and turned to look back at Grace. "I'm not surprised you're hungry. You've had nothing to eat by mouth for over a week, since you were brought into the unit. Once Dr. Phillips examines you, we'll see about getting you a tray of some soft foods; Jell-O, some chicken broth and maybe some ice cream. How does that sound?"

Grace managed a weak smile of thanks and nodded her head. Helen smiled encouragingly back at her, then turned, nodded at Pat, and left the room.

Pat shut the door and then quickly returned to the side of the bed. Grace was looking at her with sad, tormented eyes. She started to turn her head away, but stopped at the desperate sound of Pat's voice.

"Please don't shut me out, Grace. You know you're like a daughter to me. I only want to help you. Please talk to me. You must have a thousand questions."

Grace slowly turned her head to look at Pat. Since her parent's death four years ago, Pat had become like a mother to her. She had managed to keep the truth from Pat about the strangeness of her relationship with Justin. She was ashamed of her failure as a wife, and now there was *this* to deal with.

She saw in Pat's eyes what she always saw and felt she did not deserve: unconditional love. How and why Pat loved her she would never understand. Drawing a deep breath, she asked softly, "What day is it?"

Pat smiled like an excited child being rewarded for a good deed. "It's Wednesday, June 21st. You were brought in here a week ago this past Friday. So, I guess that means you will have been here two weeks day after tomorrow."

Her voice faltered and she quickly brushed a tear from her cheek. Grace stared straight ahead at the wall. She could not quite make out the design in the wallpaper that started about half way up the wall from the floor and went to the ceiling.

"Where is Justin?" she asked in a

12

flat, dull voice.

Pat walked around the end of the bed and sat down on the gray vinyl chair. Her voice sounded drained and tired. "He's at the office right now. He came here straight away the day you were brought in and didn't leave till the doctors were able to tell him that you were probably going to be all right, even though you were in a coma. They said the sooner you came out of the coma, the better your chances were for a full recovery." Pat's voice broke as she leaned back in the chair and closed her eyes. It was a full minute before she could continue. "I've been so worried. I've been staying over night for the last four nights. I wanted to be here when you woke. Justin has come by every day, but doesn't stay long. I mean, you were still in a coma and he is carrying a full caseload right now at the office. I was going to call him and let him know you were awake, but the nurse said she would up-date him on your condition."

Grace closed her eyes, trying to stop the tears that threatened to spill uncontrollably down her cheeks. She could feel herself beginning to tremble. *Justin came every day? Why? I know he HATES me, so why would he come?* Suddenly she felt Pat's gentle hand on her forehead and a soft tissue wiping the tears from her cheeks.

"Go ahead and cry, honey. Maybe that will help. I don't claim to understand this thing between you and Justin, but he was pretty shook up over this. Maybe things will start to get better. Lord knows I've been praying hard enough about it." Pat paused as she felt Grace stiffen at the mention of prayer. She sighed softly and turning sat down again. *Dear Lord,* she prayed silently, *please help my little Grace. She's troubled, Lord, troubled, broken and hurting and I don't know how to help her. But You do. Please bring her and Justin through this, and draw them back to You. Amen.*

Pat sat in silence for several minutes, and then looked up to see that Grace had fallen asleep. Brushing tears from her own face, she leaned back and closed her eyes to try and get some much-needed rest.

Dr. Evans came in almost an hour after Dr. Phillips had finished his examination. He decided on a couple of tests, but said it would be all right for Grace to start eating, and ordered the IV removed and the catheter. Dr. Evans was very gentle with Grace, trying to get her to talk about why she had suddenly felt so desperate. Hadn't their sessions been going well? Had something happened? Did she want to talk about it? Was she still feeling desperate?

Grace tried to explain to her it wasn't so much that the sessions had not been going well, but that she just could not tell her the truth about Justin. How do you discretely explain an almost every night sick perverted sex ritual? Are there any words that could adequately portray how she felt crouched in a corner as Justin lay snoring in the dark after he had finished "relieving" himself with her? Yesterday's dirty stinking garbage didn't even come close.

She had long ago given up trying to talk to him about it. Her efforts always bounced back at her like a tennis ball hitting a brick wall. He would look at her with that patient, condescending look and remind her they

14

had already discussed the matter. She was just "not remembering" for some reason. Go rest he would say, and smile as he turned and walked away from her. Was she losing her mind? She could not remember talking to him before about what was bothering her. What was wrong with her memory?

At first, when the talking failed she had tried to fight him. She stopped fighting when she realized that it only heightened his pleasure and excitement.

Grace was alone after Dr. Evans left. Pat had gone home to shower and change, promising to return later that evening. She tried to rest on her side with her arm under her head staring out the window. Thoughts and questions churned inside her. *How did this happen to me? How did my life become such a mess? What choices did I make that brought me to THIS?*

The thought that she would soon have to face Justin made her tremble. She tried desperately to get her thoughts together so that she could feel a little prepared for the coming ordeal. She closed her eyes, trying to will herself to calm down, to be able to think clearly. A tear crept down her cheek as her mind drifted back to her parents.

Godly parents had raised her, though a lot of good that had done her. It certainly had not guaranteed she made good choices; nor had it cemented a relationship with God. Somehow, she had got caught up in the "ride" of life. She kept thinking everything was just fine. She had been totally blind to what was really happening.

Maybe what was happening was due to unseen traps and attacks from Satan. After all, she did believe that there was a Holy God out there, somewhere. She had seen too much, first hand, not to believe that. And, if there was a God then there had to also be an enemy – Satan, whose sole plan was to destroy everyone.

Her problem with all of this was she felt God was unapproachable. He somehow was not listening to her any more. She had made so many mistakes, so many bad choices. He probably didn't care any more. That was partly why she felt so worthless.

How disappointed her parents would be if they could see her now. Fresh tears flowed anew down her cheeks. Both had been killed in a tragic car accident four years ago. Had it really been that long? Was that when the bottom started falling out of her world? She could not remember any more. Grace scrubbed the tears from her cheeks, and bit her lip. She had felt for a long time that she was being punished for all her "sins." Was it her fault that her parents were gone? Was God punishing her?

Grace turned over on her back, putting her arm over her eyes. Her memories forced her back in time: back to a Christian home to parents who loved God, and truly loved her. And yet, her family had been far from perfect, by any stretch of the imagination. *Is there any such thing as a perfect family?* Her parents had had their share of problems. By today's worldly standards, their communication skills were not very effective. There were a lot of verbal fights.

Her dad, who had practically grown up in the church, had met her mother while at college. She had been working at a little diner where he had often eaten meals at while studying for the

16

ministry. She had not been a Christian, but had been drawn to this tall, handsome man who had dedicated himself to a God she did not know and could not comprehend. Against all the advice he had been given he started seeing her, and they soon fell in love. His kindness and patience and the fact that he was not "preachy" about what he believed was what finally won her to the Lord. Shortly after that, they were married. Grace had been born after three miscarriages. She had been a very welcomed addition to the little family.

Her mother's health had been frail at best, even before the pregnancies and miscarriages. After Grace's birth, her health had kept her from going back to work, even on a part time basis. Things were always tight. Tempers short. Since her dad had not finished college, getting a "church" was difficult. He ended up starting a small church in a rural mountain community. Since the church was small, it could not totally "support" a minister. Her dad had also worked driving a school bus and as a night watchman at the local meat packing plant.

Because her health had always been poor, her mother had become accustomed to people focusing on and meeting her needs. It was a difficult transition to make, having to deal with a husband who was working a full time job, writing a sermon, or visiting a sick church member. He had little time for anything else, especially her or their little family. She had no comprehension or understanding of the duties of a "preacher's" wife. It was all new to her, and very overwhelming.

Grace had haunting memories of crouching on the cold wood floors of their small tenant house in the projects. From behind her closed bedroom door she would listen to their angry words thrown like lethal weapons. Back and forth, back and forth they would fly, between the two most important people in her life.

It was not always "bad." Her parents really were very good parents who deeply loved her. They just had their share of ups and downs in life. They made mistakes, just like every one else, but they did the best they could. She knew that now. Young children, and sometimes even older children, do not know how to process the "down times" and will take on the responsibility of those "down times." As she lay there in the hospital bed looking back over the years, Grace felt a deep compassion for and understanding of what her parents must have struggled with. Again, she felt great anguish over the heartaches she had brought to them through her own rebellious behavior.

She turned restlessly on the bed and looked up at the round black and white clock on the wall over the door. Would Justin be coming up to see her, and if so when? Would Pat get back before he came? She did not know if she could face him alone the first time.

Her mind drifted back to her patchy, tormented childhood memories. It is strange, but no matter how hard you try to protect your children and try to keep them safe, sometimes-bad things still happen to them. Grace rubbed her eyes hard, wishing she could block the pictures that came flooding before her mind's eye. Like a haunting horror film that you know what the ending is, but you cannot tear your eyes away from. You have to watch!

18

She had been at that tender age of five when it had all begun. The two brothers, Tommy and Joe, were six and eight years older than her. They lived in the last tenant house at the far end of the projects with their dad, William, and an older sister, Gretchen. Their mother had died of TB when they were very young and their sister had been trying to be a mother to them, struggling with an alcoholic father who only worked half the time.

She was not sure how it happened the first time. Her parents were so protective of her that she was rarely out of their sight. Somehow she had ended up playing in the sand pit behind their tenant house. She remembered the older sister coming out and telling the boys they had to come in for lunch soon and to not wander off. She was making a run to the post office and the company store and would be back within the hour.

She had no memory of how she ended up in the house with them. And so the molesting had begun. She had felt so special when they had said she could play with them in the sand pit. Then the invitation to come inside to play a special "secret" game, well, that really made her feel very special. She had not totally understood what they were doing. She had cried for only a few minutes when they had praised her for being brave and had promised it would not hurt much longer. She had eaten the Popsicle and threw the stick away before she got home. After all, it was her reward for their "secret" game, and she had to keep it a secret.

Grace had no memory of further interaction with the boys, but she must have, because one day much later Gretchen had caught them out in the woods. That was when she realized the "secret game" was a bad game. Gretchen had been so angry. She had hit both of the boys, hard, and they had taken off running for the house. They had looked almost comical hopping and jumping, trying to pull on their clothes as they ran. Grace remembered how surprised she had been to find herself standing there, with only her socks on, looking up at Gretchen. Gretchen's eyes blazed with heated anger. She had picked up Grace's clothes and thrown them at her, ordering her to put them on. Grace had struggled to get her clothes on as Gretchen stood over her. She had been frightened at first that Gretchen was going to hit her, too. Then words that poured from Gretchen like sharp poison arrows sent an even greater fear deep into her soul. She could still hear the cold hard voice even now, twenty-two years later.

"I don't want you to ever come over here again. You are a nasty, dirty little girl. When you die, you are going to go straight to hell! If you ever come over here again, I will tell your mother and father what a terrible little girl you are and they will send you away."

Grace had waited to go home until she had stopped crying. She did not want her mommy and daddy to ask her why she was crying. Her mind had reeled with the knowledge of what a terrible person she was. She was going to go to hell when she died.

She had only been five years old. Why had God let this happen to her? Grace turned on her side again, facing the window, and closed her eyes. She did not want to see or talk to anyone.

20

Chapter 3

Grace slowly woke from a dreamless sleep to the soft murmur of voices. She lay with her eyes shut, trying to get up the courage to roll over and face whoever was there. Was it Pat and a nurse? Was it one of the doctors and a nurse? Was it Justin? She strained her ears, trying to make out what was being said.

"I don't want to disturb her if she's resting." Justin whispered hoarsely to Pat, as he eyed the door. Pat had returned to find Justin standing beside Grace's bed, staring down at her. Justin had sensed it was Pat as soon as she had entered the room and had turned quickly away from the bed, wishing he had left five minutes earlier. Pat had tried to comfort him, and he had stiffened at her gentle touch. The confusion and hurt look that had instantly appeared on her kind old face momentarily made him ashamed of his actions and he had tried to relax and talk to her. He had to be very careful.

"She asked about you as soon as she woke up." Pat whispered anxiously, "Please talk to her Justin. She needs to see you."

Justin shook his head slightly in angry frustration, and tried to clear his throat. *She needs to see me? What about my needs?* Justin pinched the bridge of his nose with his fingers and finally whispered back, "I don't know, Pat, if it's a good idea for her to see me right now. My own feelings about this entire situation are in such turmoil. I'm not sure that her seeing me would help her at all. In fact, it just might make things worse." Justin looked past Pat to the door, wishing he could discreetly slip around her and leave.

Pat looked sadly at Justin. Grace had not moved in the bed. How could she possibly help these two young people she loved so very much? Neither seemed ready to let God fix their problems, and whom else could she advise them to turn to, but Him?

Grace had listened with growing apprehension to the whispered conversation between Pat and Justin. Fearing Justin was going to leave and come back when they could be alone, she turned over to lie facing them and opened her eyes.

Pat's face lit up and she smiled at Grace. "You're awake! Look who's here, honey!" Taking Justin by the arm, Pat turned a reluctant Justin around so Grace could see him. She gently pushed him toward the bed then took a step backwards. "I'll just step out here in the hall so you two can talk privately to each other." Pat turned and headed toward the door, not seeing the look of panic that crossed Grace's face or hearing the sharp intake of breath as Justin spun around to watch Pat leave.

Justin watched the door close softly, and sighing, turned to face his wife. Grace, pale from the response of her husband, stared for a moment at the closed door behind him then slowly lifted her eyes to Justin's face. She trembled slightly under the cold, closed gaze. Justin shifted uncomfortably from one foot to the other then finally spoke.

"So, are you feeling any better?" The lack of sincerity and warmth in his question made it impossible for Grace to respond. She lowered her eyes, biting her lip in confusion and sorrow.

22

"Are you not going to talk at all? I'm surprised you would pass up this opportunity to tell me how you felt life wasn't worth living any more since I'm such a horrible husband." Justin did not even try to hide the harsh bitterness and anger he was feeling.

Tears threatened to spill from Grace's eyes and she fought to keep them from coming. Justin hated it when she cried. Tears would only fan the flame of Justin's already growing anger and frustration with her. Clearing her throat, she spoke softly, "I'm sorry, Justin. I don't know what more to say than what I already wrote in my note to you."

Justin's eyes narrowed. "What note?"

Grace looked nervously at the closed door. "I wrote a note to you and left it on the kitchen counter."

Justin turned and walked to the door, yanking it open with such force it crashed loudly against the wall. He stepped out into the hall looking for Pat. He saw her sitting in a chair next to the nurses' station. As she glanced up at him, he motioned impatiently for her to come. Pat stood quickly, and walked over to him.

"Did you find a note to me from Grace in the kitchen?" His question was cold and demanding.

Pat was silent for a moment, thinking; then she carefully answered. "Yes Justin, I did. And I apologize for not giving it to you right away, and even more, for reading it. When I found it, I didn't know if Grace was going to make it or not. I was very scared, and then later, well, I guess I just forgot about it. I don't begin to understand what is going on between the two of you.

Neither of you have shared your feelings with me, but you have to know how very much I love both of you, and how deeply this hurts and troubles me."

Justin stood looking at her, struggling with his desire to slap her. *She is becoming a problem, the meddling old fool.* His feelings of anger and frustration with her came through loud and clear as he said in a forced voice, "Do you have the note with you?"

With a sad feeling of resignation, Pat sighed, carefully opened her purse, searched for just a moment, and then pulled out the note and handed it to Justin.

With flashing eyes, he grabbed it, and turned away from her to read it.

Justin,

I am so sorry to be writing this to you, but I don't see any other way to be able to try and explain to you why I feel I have no other course of action. All my attempts to try and talk to you about what is happening to us and how I feel have failed miserably. If this is my fault, if I have done something to cause you to treat me the way you do, I am sorry.

I am so confused, I don't know what has happened to us! Things were so different when we were first married. What happened? What changed? I feel like a complete failure as a wife. Our love making - well, I can't even call it that any more - It's more like you are living out some perverted fantasy - relieving a need, rather than expressing a feeling or sharing an intimate moment.

When I tried to talk to you about this, you told me we had already discussed it, that I was just not remembering. I feel like I am losing my mind. I can't do or say anything right, I feel like you are ashamed of me - I feel sure you do not love me, if you ever really did. I'm sure you don't want to be married any more, and the way things are between us, I can't continue to be with you.

I found the receipt for the diamond earrings. My

birthday and our anniversary passed, but I did not receive them, so I assume they were for someone else. Is this all my fault? Have I done something to drive you to this horrible degrading treatment of me?

I see no answers - no hope - nothing to live for.

I am sorry.

Grace

Justin reread the note, then folded it twice and stuffed it into his pocket. His eyes narrowed, and then he turned to look at Pat for a long moment. She waited, unflinching, under his hard gaze. Finally he turned to go back into Grace's room but paused at the door. Without turning around he spoke in a low cold voice, "If the idea ever enters your head again to "try and help" by withholding information from me, I will consider it cause for immediate dismissal." With that he opened the door and walked into Grace's room and closed the door behind him.

Pat stood staring at the door, a cold chill surrounding her heart. *All I can do is pray, Father. I can do nothing else.* Pat turned and went back to the chair by the nurses' station to wait for Justin to leave.

When Justin left the room Grace had got up off the bed, put on her robe and then returned to sit on the edge and wait. If Pat had the note, Justin would get it from her and read it and then return to verbally attack her. She could feel panic beginning to swell inside of her like a balloon ready to burst. She was already finding it hard to breath. When the door finally opened, she jumped involuntarily.

Justin stood just inside the closed door. His tall, muscular frame was an awesome sight to behold. Grace shivered remembering how lucky she had felt when he had first started paying attention to her in class at the University. She had only been eighteen years old, in her sophomore year, and had thought at first that he was doing it for a joke, but then he started seeking her out outside of class. She couldn't believe her luck.

He had been so kind and interesting, gentle and patient; and *he* had been interested in *her*, in what she thought, what she was doing, how she felt about things. They would talk for hours on end, about anything and everything. Their first real date had been a football game. They had cheered the home team together and thrown popcorn at each other. The next afternoon they had gone to the county fair. The crisp autumn afternoon and evening were perfect as they walked around, hand in hand, looking at the many different farm animals. They looked over all the 4-H projects and climbed on the tractors. Supper had consisted of warm crunchy corn-dogs and sticky soft cotton candy, washed down with Lemon-Shake-Up's and thick chocolate shakes. Justin had shown off his skill at the shooting booth and won her a little stuffed cocker spaniel dog, and then they had gone on several rides.

It had been a perfect evening and had ended with him walking her back to her dorm. They had stood outside until she was chilled and had to go in, but not before he had asked if he could kiss her goodnight. He had *asked* her! She had not answered. Instead, she had smiled; her lips slightly parted, and then quickly lowered her eyes. He had gently lifted her chin so she was forced to look at him, and then he had very gently kissed her. It had been the sweetest kiss she had ever had.

26

So WHAT had happened?

She could still remember those wonderful days. They could not be together often enough; walks in the woods, going to the on campus theater to see "The Sound of Music", studying together in the library, or watching television in the student lounge. It was the night of the Homecoming dance that Grace discovered that she was in love with Justin, and that *he* was in love with her. They had talked and laughed, and danced and danced and danced. They sang the songs to each other that they were dancing to. When Grace slipped on some spilled punch and almost fell, Justin had caught her and held her close. They had both been startled and a little scared. As he held her crushed to him, both their hearts had pounded and they had lost themselves in a passionate kiss.

Justin had whispered desperately in her ear, "I love you, Grace!" They had somehow ended up at his off-campus apartment. Almost before she knew what had happened, they were in his bed. After they had made love, she had turned away from him and cried. He had been confused and had pulled her to him, his strong muscular arms a comfort to her. It was then that she told him about being abused as a child. He had held her close, stroking, almost petting her, and reassuring her that he really did love her.

The next few days were scary for her. She had been sure that everything would stop between her and Justin. Instead, he had asked her to come home with him over Thanksgiving. She had called her parents to tell them that she was going to a "college friend's" home for the short Thanksgiving weekend, but she would definitely be coming home for the longer Christmas holiday. They had been disappointed but understood it was a long way to come for just a couple of days.

  Justin's family only lived an hour an a half away, compared to the fifteen hours difference from her folks, so they had left early Thursday morning and had arrived to a very warm welcome from his big family. Grace was amazed at what a large family he had: three brothers, two older and one younger, and a sister, still in high school. Both of his parents were tall, with just a hint of gray starting to show in their rusty red hair that the whole family shared. The Thanksgiving holiday was a big affair for his family: with aunts and uncles, cousins and grandparents all coming together for a big family Thanksgiving Day dinner. Grace had tried very hard not to be nervous, but had still ended up losing her breakfast.

  The family had welcomed her warmly. By the end of the weekend she had relaxed and really felt accepted.

  Justin drove the thirteen and a half hour drive over the Christmas holiday to spend a couple of days with her and meet her family and then took her back with him to his folks until they had to go back to school the first of the year. He had talked privately with her dad while at her house. When they arrived at his folks, he had given her a beautiful diamond ring. She had been amazed that he really wanted to marry her. She had convinced herself that because of all the things that had happened to her, well, she did not deserve anything good to happen in her life. Besides who would want her, wasn't she used goods?

28

She could still remember how she had sat and stared at the ring in the soft black velvet box he held out to her. He had even knelt down on one knee when he asked her to marry him. She had just sat there, tears running down her cheeks, unable to even speak. He had smiled as he gently took her hand and slipped the ring on her finger, telling her softly how he had asked her father for permission, and he had given it.

Grace could not believe that her father had not spoken to her about it, but then realized that he had probably known Justin wanted it to be a total surprise. Still, she knew her "preacher" daddy, how careful he was. He had not talked to her at all about Justin. He had not asked his usual barrage of questions; "Is he a born again Christian? What church does he belong to? How long have you known him? Does the 'Fruit' of his life bear witness to his words?" She had wondered what Justin had said to her dad to ease his mind. She herself did not know for sure if Justin was a Christian or not. To her knowledge he did not swear, smoke, or drink - you know all those things that we call "sin."

Despite her misgivings, Grace had accepted the ring and the wedding date had been set. The fact that they were actually getting married had only partly relieved her guilty conscience for having been intimate sexually with Justin prior to their being married. Maybe, since they were getting married, God would not look upon her as a fornicator. The fact was, though, she was. Marrying Justin was not going to change that. Only repentance would.

For all her "Christian" upbringing, she still could not see

that, if we let him, Satan will whitewash every obvious sin. He is so good at making us feel sorry for ourselves. Giving us excuses for all the wrong choices that we make. He is not called the Father of all liars for nothing.

Deep in her heart Grace knew she had been running from God for a while, refusing to go to the Christian college that her father had attended. She had seen too much heartache associated with "the ministry" to ever go in that direction. No, "the ministry" was not for her. She had received a scholarship at sixteen from the university to study architectural design, graduating two years ahead of her high school classmates. So she embraced the lie, convinced that she was doing the best she could to be a "good little Christian."

Grace's mind jerked back to the present as she looked up into the cold hard face of her husband, his voice just as icy. "If you think this little half ass attempt at suicide is going to manipulate me to jump through your hoops, you can think again! Be warned, I will not allow you to ruin my reputation with your sorry little act of helplessness and worthlessness. You are not smart enough or disciplined enough to win at this game. You will lose." Without another word, Justin turned and walked out of the room.

Grace sat staring after him, dazed, as if the wind had been knocked out of her. Waves of hopelessness washed over her like the pounding surf. *GOD! God, are you out there? If you are, do you even see or care about what is happening? Are you punishing me?* Dropping her head in despair, burning tears streamed down her cheeks. Suddenly the door opened. As she raised her head, Grace looked up to find Pat standing just inside the door. There was a look of sorrow and compassion on her tired, work worn face. Grace began to sob as Pat quickly came to the bedside, sat down and took her in her arms to try and comfort her breaking heart.

Chapter 4

Grace tossed restlessly on the hard hospital bed. She woke from a recurring nightmare, only to be confused by the unfamiliar surroundings for a moment. Memory slowly engulfed her, bringing with it the anguish and heartache of the day. Pat had offered to stay all night again, but her eyes betrayed the weariness in her body and mind. Grace had insisted on her going home and getting a good night's sleep. Now as she tossed and turned on the bed, she wished she had agreed to her staying. She longed for comforting arms to hold her.

Grace closed her eyes trying to will herself back to sleep. Instead her mind worked its way back in time to another childhood memory. She was back in the first grade, old Mrs. Beeker's class. Mrs. Beeker was a tall, skinny woman who had married in her late thirties and had never had children of her own. Her husband had died only two short years after their marriage, so she had gone back to work as a schoolteacher. She was strict, and would not tolerate any tomfoolery in the classroom. She was fierce with her discipline too.

Grace could still remember it like it was yesterday, the day she had felt the wrath and cruelty of this strange and hurting adult. The class had been assigned a page to work on in their math books. Grace was struggling to concentrate. Jake Williams, who sat behind her, kept poking her in the back with his pencil. Grace knew he was making marks on her blouse and besides that, it hurt! She had finally turned around and asked him to stop.

Mrs. Beeker had pounced on her like a hungry tiger. She had loudly announced to the entire class that Grace would be severely punished for talking in class and causing a distraction for the other students. She was not allowed to explain about Jake, who giggled into his hand over the trouble she was in for talking to him.

When the bell rang announcing recess, Grace had remained in her seat, fearing what was going to happen to her. The classroom had emptied amazingly fast as Mrs. Beeker had walked over to the windows that ran the entire length of the classroom. She stood with her ruler in hand, arms folded, frowning at Grace. Finally, as if she had been waiting for just the right moment, she ordered Grace to come to her. Grace had slowly risen and walked obediently over to her. She stood with her head down trying not to cry.

Mrs. Beeker had then instructed her to climb up onto a chair and to face the classroom, with her back to the windows. She was then told to pull her underpants down and bend over, so she could be spanked. Grace shook with fear and shame. Mrs. Beeker then proceeded to spank her bare bottom with the ruler. When she was finished, Grace was sobbing from the pain. As she straightened up to pull up her underpants, she looked over at the window. Lined up the full length of the windows were the entire class, laughing, pointing, and watching the whole thing. Grace jumped down from the chair and ran to the bathroom.

As she walked home alone that afternoon, she was very thankful that Mrs. Beeker had not sent a note home to her parents telling of the discipline. Having her parents find out what had

34

happened would have been the most terrible thing in the world. She remembered arriving home and complaining of not feeling well and going to bed.

But this is where her memory did strange things to her. The next morning, or so she had thought, she had awakened and went to school. All the way to school she had dreaded going for fear of the teasing she would have to put up with from the other kids. She had walked slowly, arriving just before the bell rang. As she opened the door to the first grade classroom, Mrs. Beeker looked up startled from her desk and asked her what she wanted.

Grace became confused, not recognizing anyone in the classroom and wondering why someone was sitting at her desk. Mrs. Beeker had finally stood up and walked over to her, turned her around and instructed her to go to her own class; Miss Aims' second grade room, just two doors down the hall. Grace opened the door to the room just as the bell rang. There was only one empty desk. The room was full of her classmates who did not even bother to look up when she came through the door.

Miss Aims had smiled at her and told her to take her seat and to get out her reader. Grace sat down at the only empty desk and lifted the top to see if there was a reader somewhere inside. She did not recognize any of the books in the desk. Suddenly goose bumps formed on her arm. Slowly she looked up to see the tear off calendar hanging at the far corner of the black board. The date read *February 7, 1969,* over a year in time had passed since she had gone to bed the night before. How could that be?

Grace rolled over on her back and

35

stared up at the ceiling. The large lost segment of time was still a mystery today. At twenty-seven years of age, Grace still had no memories of that time, nothing. She went to bed one night and woke up over a year later. She had not told Dr. Evans about the lost time. She did not think it had ever happened again, anyway, not for as long a time period. Maybe Justin was right, perhaps they had talked about things and she just could not remember because of a loss of time.

Grace was stiff from lying so long. She swung her legs around so she could sit on the edge of the bed. She put on her soft fuzzy house slippers and long flannel robe that Pat had brought to her and walked quietly to the door. She glanced down the hall to the nurses' station. The clock in her room read 1:20. She wondered if her nurse, Helen, was still there or if she had gone home. If she could just walk the halls for a little while maybe she could go back to sleep and not dream.

Why did she have to dream so much? It was always the same nightmare, over and over again. She was sitting in a room where there was a big screen and on the screen were scenes of the different abuses that had happened to her. Always, there was a faceless man in a long coal black coat talking to another man sitting high up on a platform. The man in the long black coat was shouting accusations, about her. It was always the same. What a terrible, awful, dirty person she was, and how she deserved to go *straight to HELL!* She could never make out the faces of either man, but she would tremble with fear and always wake up crying.

It's funny, Grace thought - well

maybe not so funny, but once a person is abused, somehow it just keeps on happening, over and over again. Almost like a pattern of behavior that gets started and then the person becomes susceptible to that type of behavior from other people. No matter how terrible it may be, it is something that slowly becomes familiar. So each time it happens they just close their mind to it a little more. Eventually it is something that is happening to them, but not really. Maybe the people who are abusive can somehow sense that in another person. It obviously did not work the other way for her. She never had a clue until after the fact that she had been dealing with an abusive person.

That was the heartbreaking thing about Justin. She had not had a clue about his hidden nature. The behavior had been sporadic the first two and a half years of their marriage. At times she had even thought that maybe she imagined it. It was only the last four years, since the death of her parents, that it started happening so often and had become so intense she could not ignore it any longer. When she would try to talk to him, it somehow always got twisted around to the point that she had begun to doubt her sanity. She had tried for a while to fight him, but she stopped when she realized the fighting only heightened his excitement and twisted pleasure in the perverted acts. She had finally reached the point of such hopelessness and intense feelings of worthlessness that she had chosen suicide as her only answer.

Grace rubbed her eyes, trying to stop the train of thoughts that had overtaken her. It was not going to help rehashing her past. She was not sure there was help out there. The phone rang at the nurses' station and was answered by a woman who said she was Phyllis. So Helen must have gone home at 11:00. Grace sighed and turned back into her room. She had felt earlier that afternoon that Helen was someone she could talk to, maybe tomorrow.

Grace slowly walked back over to the bed, took off her robe, and laid it across the end of the bed. Lying on her back, she stared up at the ceiling again. She stiffened as the silence of the night was cut by the shrill scream of a woman somewhere down the hall. She turned on her side with her back to the door allowing the heaviness of her mind to will her eyes shut. Why didn't she let Pat spend the night?

Grace showered after breakfast the next morning. The warm pulsating water soothed her aching body and softened her dry skin. She was thankful Pat had brought a few of her own things to her. Putting on real clothes instead of the awful blue dotted gowns the hospital supplied was a blessing. She was brushing her long sandy blond hair when she heard Pat's voice out in the hall by the nurses' station.

"Why can't I go in and talk to her?" Pat's voice was shaking with emotion.

"Please, Mrs. Feldman, I am going to have to ask you to leave. There has been a visitor restriction placed on Mrs. Anderson's chart. That's all I can tell you."

"A visitor restriction, by whom?" her voice rose in anger.

"I'm sorry, Mrs. Feldman, but I am not allowed to release any information concerning patients to non-authorized people." Sudden overwhelming fear rose up in Grace like a violent tidal wave. The nurse had just started to come out from the nurses' station and was trying to direct Pat back to the door of the unit as Grace hurried out into the hall.

On seeing Grace, Pat pulled her arm free from the nurse and hurried toward her. The tone of Grace's voice matched the alarm that radiated from her face. "Pat? Why can't you come and see me?"

The name on the badge that the nurse wore said Ann Hopkins. She quickly hurried past Pat, and took Grace by the arm and led her back to her room. "Please wait in your room, Grace, Dr. Evans should be here soon."

Once Grace was in her room, Ann pulled the door shut behind her and then locked it. Grace spun around as she heard the door lock and began pounding on the door. "Please. Please unlock this door! Please let me out of here. I want to see Pat!"

Pat stood staring, open-mouthed at the nurse. Ann turned from Grace's door and said very calmly, "Please, Mrs. Feldman, don't make me call security."

Grace continued to plead with the nurse from behind her locked door. Her pleas were interspersed with sobs as she continued to pound on the door. Pat's emotions rocked back and forth between anger and fear. "Please, I don't understand why the sudden restriction. I've spent several nights with her, for crying out loud! Can't you see how much you are upsetting her? Please let me go in there with her!"

Ann had now taken hold of Pat's arm and was gently, but firmly, walking her toward the door to the unit. "Please, Mrs. Feldman, I'm sorry for your confusion, but I am not allowed to discuss this with you. Please leave, so I can go in and try to help Grace."

Almost before she knew what had happened, Pat found herself standing outside the locked unit door. Fear gripped her heart, and she decided to wait till Dr. Evans or Justin arrived.

Emma Jones, another nurse on the Psyche Unit hurried out into the hall from another patient's room. "What's going on Ann?" she asked, concern showing on her face.

Ann sighed, shaking her head. "You know from report this morning, that Mr. Anderson called during the night and had a visitor restriction placed on Grace's chart. When Mrs. Feldman showed up this morning, I had to tell her I couldn't let her see Grace. Grace heard us talking and came out into the hall and I had to put her back in her room and lock the door. That's why she's carrying on like she is right now. Then I had to escort Mrs. Feldman off the unit. What a mess. I can't believe he put a restriction on Mrs. Feldman. Why, she's like a mother to that girl! I don't understand what he's trying to do, but I'll tell you what I think. I think he's up to no good!"

Emma stood for a moment listening to Grace's sobs and then looked at Ann. "Are you going in there to try and talk to her?"

Ann sighed again. "I suppose I should. I had a feeling something like this was going to happen so I called Dr. Evans right after Grace got in the shower. Just to give her a heads up, you know? And surprise, surprise, Mr. Anderson had called her last night, too. She was already getting ready to come in to the hospital when I spoke to her.

She should be here any minute." Ann looked over at the unit door where Pat was still standing outside looking in at them. "Maybe I should call her again on her car phone to let her know what has happened and to let her know that Mrs. Feldman is waiting outside the unit door."

Emma nodded, "Sounds like a plan to me. I'm going back to Anthony's room. I was just about to shave him when I heard all the commotion. I thought I should see if you needed any help."

"Thanks, I appreciate it, but I think I have it all under control." Ann turned and headed for the nurses' station "Dr. Evans should be here soon. I'll just give her a quick call and then go in to Grace and see if I can calm her down a little bit.

Grace was crumpled in a heap on the cold linoleum floor, just inside her door, sobbing. She had an overwhelming premonition that something really bad was about to happen. Something told her it would be Justin's doing, whatever it was. Her gut told her that he had put the restriction on what visitors she could have. She was too scared to even hazard a guess as to what his purpose in doing so could possibly be. Dr. Evans had not mentioned at all when she was in yesterday just how long she was going to be kept here. She had been hoping to go home as soon as the test results were in later today. This new development made her feel very uncertain about her future.

What scared her most was that Justin really knew the law and how to make it work for his benefit. What could he possibly be planning?

Moments later Grace heard the key

41

turn in the lock of her door. Scrambling to her feet she turned to see Ann slowly open the door and come in, gently shutting it behind her. Ann stood with her back to the door for a second, just looking at Grace, compassion reflecting from her large dark brown eyes. Then she cleared her throat and spoke, "Grace, can we sit down for a minute and talk?"

Grace had involuntarily stepped backwards when she saw that it was not Pat coming into the room. She stood silently looking at Ann, wondering if she was friend or foe. Finally, she nodded her head and walked over to her bed. She climbed onto the bed and sat cross-legged in the middle looking at Ann expectantly.

Ann heaved a sigh of relief and walked over to sit at the foot of the bed. She paused only for a moment and then began, "I'm sorry for all the confusion this morning, Grace. When we had report this morning at shift change, there were some new orders on your visitor allowance. I don't know any more than that, so there really isn't a whole lot more I can tell you. You're welcome to ask me questions. I will try to answer them as best I can, but I really don't have any more information."

Grace was silent, looking at Ann. A lump formed in her throat. For a moment she could not speak. She turned her head to look out the window, and tried to think what possible question she could ask that Ann would be able to answer. Ann waited patiently. Finally Grace turned to look at Ann. Very slowly she asked her question, "Was it Justin who put the restriction on my visitors?" She watched Ann's face closely for any sign of deception.

42

Ann's mind raced as she tried to keep all emotion from her face. She knew there would be no way to keep the truth from Grace. She also knew that trying to say she believed Justin's reasons for the restriction were for her own good would never be believed, as she did not believe that herself.

For a brief second, even though she was trying not to let it happen, Ann's face reflected her frustration with the whole situation. The look was so fleeting that for a moment Grace was not sure she had really seen it. Then Ann slowly spoke.

"Grace, I wish I had some answers for you. Yes, Justin asked for the restrictions to be put in place, and Dr. Evans also approved the restriction. I really wish there was more that I could tell you, but I just don't have any answers."

The sincerity Grace heard in Ann's voice only made her heart sink deeper into despair. Her mind rushed back to the previous evening and the cold hard words Justin had spoken to her. . . .

"If you think this little half ass attempt at suicide is going to manipulate me to jump through your hoops, you can think again! Be warned, I will not let you ruin my reputation with your sorry little act of helplessness and worthlessness. You are not smart enough or disciplined enough to win at this game. You will lose."

Grace was jerked back to the present as Ann reached out a hand to touch her arm. "Don't lose hope, Grace. Dr. Evans is on her way in and I'm sure she will be able to answer all your questions."

Grace sat staring out the window as her tears fell unchecked down her cheeks. She could not make herself believe that anything would ever be OK again.

Chapter 5

Grace was still trying to understand what Dr. Evans was saying when Ann tapped on the door and announced that Judge Parker had arrived.

Dr. Evans sighed and turning to Grace, gave her an encouraging smile. "It's going to be alright, Grace. Trust me."

Grace slowly followed Dr. Evans out of her room and down the hall to a room that the staff used to give report at shift change. As Grace entered the room, she was not surprised to see Justin sitting at the far end of the table. A woman in a black robe that Grace assumed was Judge Parker stood talking with Dr. Phillips and Ann Hopkins, the charge nurse. Grace swallowed hard, trying to calm herself and not lose her breakfast. Dr. Evans took her arm and guided her to a chair and they both sat. Grace glanced nervously over at Justin; she wanted to make sure she could look away quickly if he happened to look at her. She knew she should talk to him, but she was also desperately afraid to. She did not need to worry; he kept his eyes focused on the piece of paper in front of him on the table. He seemed to be reading it and did not look up or over at her.

Grace felt uneasiness churning up inside her. She reviewed in her mind what Dr. Evans had told her only a few short minutes before.

"Grace, Justin told me that you have been losing time. I sat up last night reviewing my notes from all our sessions. I would really like for you to see a specialist. I feel he should be able to help you with the condition that I am beginning to think you just

might have.

It's hard to explain and I don't want you to think that you have done anything wrong. This is really good news. I'm thinking we might be close to a breakthrough for you.

Because the doctor I want you to see only works with patients on an in-patient basis, you will need to be transferred to another facility. He only treats patients on a three-month commitment. So, that means you will be at this other facility a minimum of three months. Believe me, the time will go fast, and I will come and see you once a week.

Justin doesn't think you will agree to the three-month commitment, so he has brought in a Judge. He really wants you to get the help you need so the two of you can get on with your lives together. He really does love you, Grace. He's been very upset over this whole thing."

Grace rubbed her forehead and looked over at Justin. He was still reading or studying the paper in front of him. He did not look up or over at her, not even once. Suddenly, the Judge turned and looked in the direction of her and Dr. Evans. She was tall with chestnut colored hair, graying slightly at the temples. As she pulled out a chair to sit down, she addressed Dr. Evans. "Is everyone here, Dr. Evans?"

Dr. Evans stood, clearing her throat, "Yes your honor. We're ready to begin."

Judge Parker sat down and a woman that Grace had not noticed before sat next to her and began typing on a small machine. Judge Parker looked directly at Grace for a moment, and then spoke in a slightly condescending tone of voice,

"Mrs. Anderson, do you understand why we are here today, and what is going on?"

Grace glanced at Dr. Evans, who suddenly looked down at her papers and began shuffling them. She paused for only a moment to look at Justin before looking back at the Judge. Judge Parker watched with interest, as Grace's face seemed to change from a look of confusion to a blank stare. Then her eyes slowly focused, and with her hands clasped tightly together she answered in a calm soft voice, "Well, I think I do. Dr. Evans said she wants me to go and see a different doctor that only treats patients on an in-patient basis under a three-month commitment. It's my understanding that Justin thinks I won't agree to the treatment, so that's why you are here. Is that correct?"

Judge Parker sat looking at Grace. She glanced over at Justin, who nodded slightly, and then turned back to Grace. "Yes, Mrs. Anderson, that is correct. What is actually transpiring here is what is commonly referred to as a competency hearing. I will ask your doctors some questions, your husband will be allowed to make a statement, and I will also ask you some questions. I will listen to all the answers and statements and make a determination if commitment to this other facility is warranted. If I decide it is, I will then decide just how you will be transported there, and for how long a duration."

Grace opened her mouth to ask her a question, but Judge Parker turned to Dr. Phillips and spoke to him. "Dr. Phillips, can you please give me your report on Grace Anderson's physical condition."

Dr. Phillips spoke quickly,

stating the specifics of Grace's physical condition. She was stable and he saw no reason why she could not be transported to another facility without any serious problems.

Judge Parker then asked for a report from Ann Hopkins the charge nurse. Ann quickly related that Grace's night had been quiet but that she had become upset this morning when a visitor was not allowed in to see her. She quickly added that Grace had also calmed down without any extraordinary measures having to be taken.

Judge Parker sat quietly for a moment reviewing her notes and taking a moment to jot something down, and then turned to Dr. Evans. "May we have your report now, Dr. Evans?"

Dr. Evans opened the folder in front of her, and clearing her throat, stated that she felt her sessions with Grace had been going well, so she was surprised and unprepared for the turn of events that brought Grace to the hospital. She said that after talking extensively with Mr. Anderson, she had come to the conclusion that it was very possible Mrs. Anderson had a condition called "multiple personality disorder."

She began by explaining a multiple personality disorder usually manifested itself due to some kind of physical, mental or emotional trauma that was buried deep in the subconscious mind. It was a way for the mind to protect itself from having to deal with the trauma.

She further explained that because the condition of multiple personalities was a coping mechanism the main personality was usually unaware of the other personalities. She explained how this could complicate treatment as a different personality could emerge and refuse treatment. She said this was why there needed to be a "commitment" in place for the treatment to have even a chance of success.

Dr. Evans further stated, "for-the-record", that "Grace", the main personality, was more than willing to undergo treatment. Unfortunately she had not been able to actually identify any other personalities to date. Nor had she been able to determine just how many there actually were. It was also her recommendation that there be a court ordered commitment in place.

Grace had been watching Justin while Dr. Evans spoke. With the last comment, for just an instant Grace saw the corners of his mouth turn up into a smile. Quickly he controlled his face back to his serious concerned look. Fear gripped her heart as she turned to look at the Judge.

Judge Parker was again making notes. The nonstop pinging of the machine the woman sitting next to the Judge was typing on was almost hypnotic. Judge Parker finally looked up from her note taking. Her gaze rested for a moment on Grace then turned to Justin. "Mr. Anderson, do you have anything to add at this point?"

Justin now glanced for the first time at Grace, his face a confusing mask of emotions. His voice broke for a second as he started to speak, and he paused as if trying to regain control of his emotions. Finally he looked up at Judge Parker and spoke, "Judge Parker, I want to apologize for my emotional display, but this whole thing has been very hard on me. I have a deep love for my wife, and this whole situation has been a shock to say the least." He paused for dramatic effect and looked over at Grace for a moment, then continued. "I have been greatly concerned for my wife for the last couple of years. She has always had a slight problem with her memory, but it seems to have intensified over the last four years, I'd say ever since the tragic death of her parents." Justin paused again to clear his throat.

Grace sat transfixed, staring wide-eyed at this total stranger.

"I have tried repeatedly to get her into some kind of counseling since that tragic event, and she only this past winter agreed to start seeing Dr. Evans. Unfortunately, Dr. Evans was not told until late last evening that Grace has been "losing" segments of time. To be perfectly honest I am afraid for Grace's safety, not to mention my own, because of this "multiple personality" thing. I have asked Dr. Evans to please help us get to the bottom of this so we can get on with our lives together." Justin turned again to look at Grace, his voice seeming to break under the emotional strain, and he continued in a gruff whisper, "My wife is very precious to me, and I don't want to take any more chances with her life!"

Grace was now trembling with shock and fright. Justin's words from the evening before again thundered in her ears, ". . . *Be warned, I will not let you ruin my reputation with your sorry little act of helplessness and worthlessness. You are not smart enough or disciplined enough to win at this game. You will lose.*"

Grace felt her throat closing up and fought for air as she griped the table. She opened her mouth to speak, to cry out, but nothing came. She looked franticly at Dr. Evans, who had put her hand on Grace's arm, asking, "Grace? Grace, are you alright?"

Judge Parker sat writing on the form in front of her for a moment. She handed it to the woman next to her, who signed and stamped it and again began typing on her machine. Judge Parker looked at Grace. Finally she asked, "Do you have anything that you would like to add, Mrs. Anderson?"

Grace struggled to collect her frantic thoughts, then suddenly looked up calmly at the Judge and spoke, "Your honor, I really don't think I have that serious an issue with my memory or this loss of time thing. I am, however, having a hard time believing the sincerity of my husband's words. His actions for just the last several months alone have been much different from what he has just stated so melodramatically to you. I do want to see this specialist, if for no other reason than to prove that there is nothing wrong with me. But I have to voice my objection to this kangaroo hearing and the greatly exaggerated statements made by my husband."

Dr. Evans was staring wide eyed at Grace. She turned to Judge Parker, and smiling said, "Judge Parker, I believe we have just witnessed a demonstration of another personality in Grace. She has never and would never speak in such a manner. She is much too reserved and shy to speak out like this."

Before Grace could make another comment, Judge Parker spoke, "Well, be that as it may, I have already made my decision. I am hereby ordering a court committal of no less than ninety days at Western State Hospital in Lakewood, Washington. A release prior to the ninety-day commitment will have to be approved by me. Transport will be by Washington State Police and will take place day after tomorrow, Saturday, June 24th."

The loud banging of the gavel on the table made Grace jump. She turned frightened eyes to Dr. Evans. "Dr. Evans, don't I get to say anything?"

Dr. Evans leaned in close to her, "What do you mean? You just made a very dramatic statement." She looked nervously over at Justin who had risen and walked around the table to talk to Judge Parker. She turned quickly to Grace, "Don't worry, Grace. Every thing is going to be OK. This is really for the best. That's all any of us want really, for you to get better, and this is the quickest way."

Judge Parker's assistant slid a form in front of Grace. "Mrs. Anderson, I need you to sign and date both places that are marked with an X."

The piece of paper blurred before Grace's eyes. She looked at the assistant with blank eyes and then turned to Dr. Evans, unsure of what she was signing. "Go ahead Grace, sign it. It's just the formal paper work for the commitment. It just states everything that Judge Parker just said. It's OK."

Grace numbly signed the paper. She looked up to see Justin watching her. She stood quickly as he smiled at her. Suddenly he came around the table and putting his arm around her kissed her on the cheek. Grace began to tremble violently under his touch. As she tried to step away from him the room seemed to tilt and suddenly she was engulfed in merciful blackness.

Grace opened her eyes to find herself lying on the bed in her hospital room. Dr. Evans was standing by the door talking to Ann the charge nurse. Grace could tell by the frustrated sound of Ann's voice that something was troubling her.

Dr. Evans sighed nervously. "Well, it's too late now to say anything. Whatever happens, it really is in Grace's best interest to go to Western State for evaluation and treatment."

Grace sat up on the bed and quickly got to her feet. Dr. Evans turned from Ann and walked toward her as she blurted out, "Dr. Evans, please, may I see my housekeeper, Pat?"

Dr. Evans looked back at Ann, and then turned back to Grace. "Well, Grace, Justin felt it was anti-productive for you to have visits from Pat. She did after all keep your note to Justin. She really should have given it to him immediately."

"She was scared, Dr. Evans! I almost died. She probably just forgot about it." Grace's voice was beginning to sound agitated.

Dr. Evans sighed. "OK, I'll talk to Justin. I personally don't see any harm in you seeing Pat. I'm sure I can talk him into letting her come see you before you leave for Western. OK?"

Grace nodded helplessly, tears now soaking her cheeks. What would she do if she could not see Pat again? She felt like she was about to disappear off the face of the earth and no one would know or care.

"Your lunch is here. Do you think you could eat something?" Dr. Evans smiled encouragingly.

"Will you talk to Justin right away?" Grace pleaded, wiping the tears from her cheeks.

"Yes, Grace. I'll go and call him right now. Try to eat something and I'll be back first thing tomorrow morning." Dr. Evans headed for the door of the unit, leaving Ann to steer Grace to the day room where the lunch trays were being put on the tables by the kitchen staff.

Grace paused at the day room door to watch Dr. Evans leave. A shiver of apprehension ran down her back like a cold icicle on a hot sticky summer afternoon. She did not believe Dr. Evans. Something told her nothing was ever going to be OK again.

Three hours later found Grace pacing the day room as she waited anxiously for Pat to come. The shift change had just taken place and she was hoping that Helen was going to be her nurse again for the evening. Maybe she would know if Dr. Evans had reached Justin, and if Pat would be coming that evening to see her.

She sank exhaustedly into a large, overstuffed rocker and put her head back, closing her eyes. She thought about Pat, her dear sweet housekeeper. Pat, the first adult she had trusted since her parent's death. Pat had become more like a mother to her than an employee. Tears flowed down her cheeks. She really needed to talk to Pat. She was so scared right now, she did not know if she could face going all the way to Spokane under police escort. What exactly did that mean anyway?

Grace sat with her eyes shut, slowly letting the gentle rocking of the chair calm her shattered nerves. The heaviness of fatigue settled over her like warm blankets on a cold winter's evening, and she drifted off into a restless sleep.

Chapter 6

Grace could hear the soft gentle notes of the piano as her voice teacher played for her. She was only nine years old, but her parents had wanted her to have private voice lessons. They had moved the year before from the small mountain community to a fairly large community in eastern Montana. The church that her dad had been sent to had a fairly good size congregation. Her mother, who was feeling much better, had decided she wanted to go back to work. An older couple in the church offered to take care of Grace after school. The older gentleman, a retired voice teacher, offered to give Grace singing lessons since she seemed to have a natural talent.

At first she had enjoyed the attention, and it was fun singing and learning new songs, how to breathe and hold notes, how to sing from her tummy and not from her throat.

Then, one day, while the woman was at the store, she and the man sat together at the piano and practiced her song for Sunday. Sitting there side-by-side on the piano bench, she suddenly noticed his pants were open in the front, and something was hanging out. When he reached over and took her hand and placed it in his lap, she suddenly felt like her throat was going to close. As he guided her hand to grasp hold of him, he continued with the lesson as if nothing out of the ordinary was going on. Grace struggled to keep her voice steady. Carefully he guided her hand to slide up and down. After several minutes, he released his hold on her hand and turned away from her, grabbing up a towel that lay on the bench beside him. Covering himself for a moment he jerked silently then dropped his head, shaking slightly. Grace sat silently beside him waiting for him to begin playing again.

In a quiet voice he spoke to her. "Grace, dear. You are a precious young lady. You are so very special to me. I want you to know that we will every now and then, have a special time like this together. It's so special, that I don't want anyone else to share in our special time. This will be just between you and me." He turned to look at her. "Do you understand what I am saying to you, dear?"

Grace sat looking from his kindly old face to his lap. Her mind reeled with confusion. She looked again into his kindly old eyes and slowly nodded her head.

He smiled a gentle smile and reached out his hand to touch her face. "You are a good little girl, Grace."

Why am I a "good little girl" now, but a "nasty, dirty little girl" with Tommy and Joe? She did not understand.

Grace jerked awake at the gentle touch on her arm. "Grace?" Grace opened her eyes to see Helen standing beside the chair. "Are you OK? You were crying and moaning in your sleep."

Why, why did she keep having this same dream? It seemed so real, like a memory, especially since Mr. Jenkins had given her voice lessons. But surely, it was just a stupid dream. Yet, she had had this same dream for as long as she could remember. She did remember there would be times when they were alone, and all she would remember was being patted on the head and told what a good little girl she was. In frustration, Grace reached up and wiped the tears from her

56

cheeks. "I'm OK. Is Pat coming to see me?" she asked.

Helen smiled and nodded her head. "Yes, she's coming this evening, after supper, for about an hour." Helen turned and pulled up a chair from the table and sat. "Feel like talking?"

Grace looked at Helen, trying to decide if she was someone she could trust or not. Helen met her gaze, waiting patiently. Grace's lip began to tremble. She quickly covered her face with her hands trying to stifle the sobs that rose in her throat and spilled from her like a gushing fountain.

Grace pulled her knees up and rested the backs of her hands on them. With her head resting on her hands, her shoulders shook from sobs. It was several minutes before she could stop crying and even then she still trembled sporadically. When Grace finally had control again, she looked up surprised to see Helen still sitting in the chair next to her. The expression on her face was not pity it was more like compassion. Grace wondered how she could have compassion for someone she did not even know.

"I'm really scared, Helen." she said, her voice barely above a whisper.

"What do you think is making you feel scared?" Helen asked as she handed Grace a couple of tissues.

Grace wiped her eyes with one and then blew her nose. She looked at Helen, trying again to determine if she was really sincere. Finally, she whispered, "I'm afraid Justin is planning something that is not really for my good. I wish I could believe that he was sincere today during the hearing, but I can't. Not after what he said to me last night."

Helen was silent for a moment then asked, "What did he say last night?"

Grace rubbed the kink in the back of her neck, closing her eyes in an effort to concentrate. Her mouth was very dry, she licked her lips and then very slowly recited Justin's parting statement from the night before.

"If you think this little half ass attempt at suicide is going to manipulate me to jump through your hoops, you can think again! Be warned, I will not let you ruin my reputation with your sorry little act of helplessness and worthlessness. You are not smart enough or disciplined enough to win at this game. You will lose."

Grace's voice broke with the last few words. The fear and panic that Helen saw in her eyes and on her face was enough to convince her that Grace's concerns were real and not an act, and possibly well founded. At shift change, Ann had expressed the same concerns. Now after hearing what Justin had said, she was anxious to be able to say something that would give her a little hope, something to hold on to.

"You know, Grace, we don't always know why things happen to us or why they happen the way they do. We can't always see the whole picture. It's kind of like that type of art that when you are looking at the painting up close, it's really hard to know or "see" what you are looking at. But when you step back, then you can get a clearer picture, and suddenly the whole thing just seems to jump out at you. It's like, WOW, what looked like just blobs of paint are now a picture of a small boy playing with his puppy."

Grace sat, eyes wide, staring at Helen, intently taking in every word.

58

Helen leaned forward slightly, and continued softly, "Things that happen to us, situations, can be just like that picture. Just blobs of painful incidents, hurt feelings, actions that cause confusion, lost hopes and dreams, abuse, just to mention a few. What helps to make the picture clear, is to step back, and see the hand that is painting the picture of your life. It's a hand that "sees" all the hurtful things, and with a brush full of love and compassion, very carefully blends all the "blobs" to make a beautiful life to be cherished and loved."

Tears fell silently down Grace's cheeks. She turned her head to look out the window. "Do you really think God cares one twit about me?" Helen could not help but hear the hurt and bitterness in Grace's voice.

Helen was silent for a moment. She longed to take Grace in her arms and tell her just how strongly she knew and believed that yes, God cared a lot more than just a twit about her. She knew she had to choose her words carefully. After a moment, she reached out and gently took Grace's limp hands in her own.

Very softly she said, "Grace, more than you could ever possibly comprehend, God knows right where you are, and even though you can not see past the "blobs", He is painting a masterpiece. Hold on to that. Hold on to Him. He won't let go of you. If you believe nothing else, believe that."

Very gently she squeezed Grace's hands then released them. Standing up, she pushed the chair back under the table. As she turned toward the door, she stopped and looked at Grace who still sat staring out the window. "I'm here till 11:00. If you want to talk, just come and get me." Ever so slightly, Grace nodded her head. *Give me the right words, Lord.* Helen prayed. *Give me Your WORDS. That's what she needs to make it through this.*

Pat came right after the supper trays had been picked up and stayed for over an hour. They sat in Grace's room talking. Pat had sadly told Grace that Justin had told her after the hearing earlier that morning that he had decided her services were no longer needed and she had spent the afternoon packing her personal things from the house. Grace had become very distraught, and cried. Pat did not tell her how Justin had stood in the door and watched her pack for almost twenty minutes before he finally got tired of waiting on her and had left to go work in his study.

Pat had slipped into the master bedroom and quickly packed a bag for Grace. She packed an assortment of her clothes along with some toilet items and a few other personal things she knew Grace would want. She also went to Grace's secret hiding place and got her journals, her private bankbook, her baby book and her photo albums. She found Grace's mother's Bible in the nightstand drawer and had brought that too, along with the few pieces of her mother's jewelry.

Grace had cried as she looked at the things Pat had thought to bring to her. Softly she asked, "Will you be OK, Pat? What will you do? I can't believe that Justin let you go!"

Pat had assured her that she would be just fine, and promised to come up to the state hospital to see her. Pat held her tightly before leaving and whispered in her ear, "I'll be praying for you,

Grace. God does love you and you are not alone!"

Grace had stood by the door for a good ten minutes after Pat left. Tears ran silently down her cheeks. Did God really love her? She had not felt loved by Him or any one, except for Pat, for a long time. She missed her parents. She wondered if she would be in the hospital right now if they were still alive. Could she have told her parents what was going on? What would have happened if she had not married Justin? Grace finally returned to her room and sat in the chair looking out the window. She leaned her head back and closed her eyes letting her mind slowly slip back in time. . . . .

Grace stood nervously adjusting her dress. Her mother had just left her to be seated in the church sanctuary. The photographer had taken a picture of little Timmy looking at her garter, and then took one of her and Emily, her best friend and maid-of-honor. Slowly the door opened and Mr. Albert, one of the church deacons said they were ready for the procession.

Emily picked up her bouquet and handed Grace's to her. Smiling she said, "This is it, Kiddo!" and turning walked out into the hall. Grace lowered her face into the beautiful bouquet of lilacs and white lilies. She breathed in deeply the pleasing fragrances, trying to swallow the lump that was forming in her throat.

As she walked toward the door, her dad suddenly came into view. His tall muscular frame filled the door and his smiling face almost brought tears to her eyes. He stood there for a moment just looking at her.

"You are one beautiful bride,

little girl. I can't believe that you are really getting married. Your mother and I are so proud of you, honey." He held out his arm for her to take and turned his head away, brushing a tear from his own eyes.

Grace slipped her arm through his and stood on tiptoe to kiss his cheek. They walked slowly toward the door of the sanctuary. Emily was already walking down the aisle. Little Timmy and Rebecca were getting last minute whispered instructions from Mr. Albert.

As Rebecca and Timmy started their slow walk down the aisle, Mr. Albert slipped into the sanctuary and sat in the back row. Grace stood silently beside her dad, waiting for the organist to give them their cue to begin their walk to the front of the sanctuary.

Suddenly, Grace heard a voice, questioning very softly in her ear. **"Grace, what are you doing marrying this man? You do not even know him!"** Startled, Grace turned to look at her father. He was looking straight ahead, trying hard to not show the emotion that was welling up inside over his little girl getting married. "Daddy, did you say something?"

David Adams turned to look at his daughter, smiled, and patted her hand, "No honey, I didn't say anything. Getting the jitters?" He chuckled softly at his little joke.

Grace felt the color drain from her face, and for a moment felt like she just might faint. Mr. Adams took hold of her arm and leaned close, "Grace, honey, are you sure you're OK?"

Grace nodded silently, and glanced around to see if any one else could have possible been close enough to ask the question. As far as she could tell,

they were the only ones in the vestibule. Who could it have been?
GOD, is that you?

Grace opened her eyes and looked over at the clock on the wall. 9:30. She stood up and walked to the door. The hall was empty and dark except for the light at the nurses' station. Grace walked down the hall to the day room and sat down in the big rocker. The television was on, but she was oblivious to its noise.

Could the voice she had heard back on her wedding day have been God? Could God have been trying way back then to get her attention? To spare her all the troubles she had since faced? Grace had to admit that on her wedding day she had not known for sure if Justin really loved her, or for that matter, if she loved him. She just knew that she had felt guilty and dirty for being with him before they had actually gotten married.

She felt she really had no choice about the matter. She had convinced herself that only by marrying Justin would she be able to justify their living together before they had married. Looking back on that time now, she could see how it had changed both of them. She now knew that if a relationship was based purely on sex it was doomed. Sex without a foundation of non-sexual intimacy does not have much of a chance of making it.

Her parents had demonstrated how having God at the center of a relationship was the binding glue that held people together. Through the good times and the bad times, that was the way God intended a marriage to work. Still, she had been unable or unwilling to see the truth.

Grace stood up and walked over to

the window. Rain was gently falling and the lights from the parking lot made the scattered puddles dance as the drops fell steadily. What would have happened that day if she had simply turned to her dad and confessed her sin of being intimate sexually with Justin; how she did not want to make it worse by marrying someone she knew God did not want her to marry?

Tears filled her eyes wetting her face again. She knew what would have happened. Her wonderful daddy would have stood by her side and whisked her out of there and helped her to get back on the right path. Even at that point, she could have started over. Instead, she had let pride keep her from acknowledging her sin. She had grabbed hold of Satan's lie about her sin and went from the frying pan right into the fire. Grace rested her head against the cool glass and sobbed. She did not hear Helen come up behind her.

As Helen stood behind Grace, listening to her sob out her sorrow and pain, she prayed silently, *"Dear God, what can I say to her? Give me the right words to reach her."* Helen stepped closer and took hold of each of Grace's upper arms and gently turned her and walked her over to the couch. Grace did not resist, but let herself be guided by Helen. When she sat down, she leaned forward. Resting her elbows on her knees, and burying her face in her hands, she continued to sob.

Helen sat opposite her without speaking. Finally, she reached over and touched Grace's arm. Grace looked up, her eyes red and swollen from crying.

"Grace, I don't know what is troubling you so greatly. I do know, whatever it is, God is bigger. He's

64

bigger than our problems, our hurts and disappointments. He's even bigger than our past. You do not have to face anything alone. But you do have to truly desire to face whatever it is and be set free through the power of Jesus Christ. If you don't I can promise you that you will spend the rest of your life putting a bandage over a festering wound that will never heal."

Pain and frustration was visible on Grace's face. "Do you think I don't want to be free of this?"

Helen smiled. "Well, it is a reasonable question. You might wonder, why would anyone not desire to be healed? Believe it or not, there are benefits in being afflicted. A person can become so accustomed to coping with the disadvantages of afflictions that those disadvantages eventually seem comfortable, even desirable. They're so used to living with the hurt and pain, they are afraid to live without it. They feel "safe" in the affliction. They're used to that whole package, know exactly what to expect, no surprises.

Sometimes, it is easier to cling to emotional wounds. Whether deserved consequences of past sins, or undeserved by things done to us; facing the feelings from those wounding experiences is not easy. There is also a fear factor involved. Facing our true feelings may be too much for us to handle. Sometimes it's easier to believe that present misery is deserved payment for past sins. Then we can reject God's forgiveness. After all, if we can accept God's forgiveness of our sin, then not only do we have to forgive ourselves, but we also have to forgive the other person or persons involved with the wounding.

This is where self-pity comes into play, a great tool of Satan. Most people would rather nurse a grudge against the offending person, make them pay and keep everyone reminded of how badly they were treated.

Also, healing would mean becoming responsible for our own decisions and the consequences of our choices. You know, what we have done with our life. Once we are healed we would no longer have a reason for not leading a more productive life. It would mean a drastic change in our life-style. That's an unknown, and therefore holds the possibility of failure. But the alternative to not truly being healed is to never be able to move on, to do/be all that God has planned for our life. That would be a tragic loss."

Grace was silent, soaking in what Helen had said. It seemed to fit her to a tee. How could Helen have known to say just what she needed to hear? Was it possible that God *did* really care about her? She knew, in her heart, that she really did love God. After all, she had asked Jesus into her heart as a child, she was a Christian. But if she was honest with herself, she knew that when situations arose that she could not deal with, instead of turning to Jesus, she had reacted in a very human way. Because of the shame she had felt, she would deny to herself that she had reacted in that awful way. She would actually go off into a fantasy. Before long she was not able to discern what was real and what was make believe.

A scripture verse she had learned when she was just a child came to mind: *"Finally, brothers, whatever things are true, whatever things are honorable, whatever things are just,* whatever things are pure, whatever things are lovely, whatever things are of good report, if there is any virtue, and if there is any praise, think about these things."*

Grace knew in her heart that she had not been following that verse very well. She finally looked up at Helen. "How do I do it?" she whispered. "How do I get healed of all my past? You don't know what all I need to be healed from."

Helen smiled. "I don't need to know Grace. God already knows. You just need to want to work with Him. That's really the first step that has to be taken to receive healing, that and the realization that time and effort are involved in the healing. You have to be active in the healing process along with Jesus. Sometime we are so distracted by all the pain and fear involved, God has to do something drastic to get our attention and involvement."

Grace stared at her tightly clasped hands. She wanted the pain to stop, but she did not know how much she could really change.

Very softly she prayed, "*God, I don't always make the right choices. You already know that. You also know how messed up my life and marriage are right now; have been for a long time. I know I've been failing miserably on my own. So, maybe, instead of me making decisions, well, maybe You could make the decisions from now on. I give up my right to choose. I give that right to You. I'm asking You to make sure I don't screw up and end up in hell. I came real close last week. For some reason, you spared me. So, You make the choices for me from now on. OK?"*

*Philippians 4:8 World English Bible

Grace didn't look up or she would have seen tears of joy streaming down Helen's face. What neither of them realized was that sometimes, to really be healed, God has to take someone all the way down, flat on their face. Then the only way they can look is up, back to Him. That was exactly what was about to happen to Grace. Her whole world was about to fall completely apart.

Chapter 7

Phyllis, the night charge nurse, woke Grace at 5:30 a.m. Saturday morning. Grace at first was confused and could not remember where she was. Memory flooded back in painful waves when Phyllis said she had to get up and get ready for transport to Western State Hospital. "The officer called and said he will be here within the hour."

"You mean, within the next hour, between now and 6:30?" Foggy from the medication she had been given the night before, Grace struggled to understand what was happening.

Phyllis set Grace's suitcase on the bed, and walked toward the door. "Yes, he said they would be here sometime between 6:00 and 6:30. Oh, you won't want to take any valuable personal items with you. I'll bring you a box you can put those things in and then we'll seal the box and you can write on it who you want authorized to come and pick it up." Phyllis paused for a moment, and then continued, "You can make one phone call, but you will need to do it soon, as you have to leave as soon as the officer gets here. OK?"

Grace stood staring at Phyllis, wide-eyed with shock and confusion. Phyllis frowned, "Did you understand what I just said?" She asked. Grace finally nodded her head, and turned to start getting dressed.

Phyllis sighed shaking her head as she thought about how they had said in report when she came on that Grace had been out-of-it most of the day Friday. She watched Grace for a minute thinking how sad it was that this young woman could be in such a messed up state of being. She turned slowly and walked out of the room.

    Grace dressed slowly, still under the heavy slow-motion effects of the medication. She had asked Dr. Evans when she came in on Friday why she had to take yet another pill. Now as she started sorting her things, trying to decide what to take with her and what to have Pat come and get, she could not remember a thing Dr. Evans had said to her. In fact, she could not remember much of the entire day. Phyllis came back in with a box and Grace put her mother's jewelry and all but one of her photo albums in the box. She packed her baby book and wedding album and private bankbook. Grace picked up her mother's worn Bible and stood for a moment looking at it. She only hesitated for a second, then turned and put the Bible on the bed to be packed with the things she was taking with her.

    Grace closed the box and sealed it with the tape Phyllis had brought in to her and wrote her name on the outside of the box. Then she wrote Pat's name and phone number on top of the box.

    After packing her suitcase and overnight bag she went out to the nurses' station and made her phone call to Pat. Pat had still been in bed and sounded sleepy to Grace, but she reassured Grace that she would come that morning to get her things and would keep them with her till she wanted them. Grace would have talked longer, but Phyllis told her that the officers were there to get her and so she said a tearful good-by, with Pat promising to come up as soon as it was allowed.

    As Grace hung up the phone she turned to see two officers standing close. As if being committed to a mental hospital wasn't bad enough, she was alternately shocked, alarmed and filled with shame at the first touch of the smooth icy cold handcuffs. She had not been prepared for that. Her body shook with fear as the officer slipped the cuffs onto her wrists.

Startled, Grace looked over at Phyllis. Uncontrollably her body began to shake. "What's going on?" she gasped.

The taller of the two officers, his deep royal blue uniform still smelling of the starch his wife must have used while ironing it, picked up her bags without comment. The other office, shorter and stockier in stature, his uniform showing signs of ware with a catsup stain above his right knee, took her by the arm and guided her out of the hospital. "This is a court committal, Mrs. Anderson, so we have to escort you this way to prevent your attempting to escape. I'm sorry for this, but it's the way it has to be. When we get you inside the van I will remove the cuffs."

Tears forcefully rushed down Grace's cheeks. She was glad no one else was up to see her being taken away in handcuffs. Comprehension that Justin had allowed something like this to be done to her washed over her like a soaking from a tub of icy water. It reinforced her conviction that there was no natural healthy love for her left in him. He must have known they would do this.

Once outside, she was put in the back of a dingy gray van that had no windows, not in the sides or the back. The older model van showed patches of rust and decay where the salt from many hard winters had eaten away at the gray metal around the wheels and along the base of the van. The officer opened the right hand back door of the van, which

71

was divided down the middle by a metal panel. One single seat ran the length of the van along the outside wall.

After helping her into the van the officer removed the handcuffs and closed the door without further comment. She felt numb with shock, as the darkness seemed to swallow her up in its thick inky blackness. The clunk of the key turning in the door brought beads of sweat to her forehead and armpits, and a feeling of nausea to her stomach. Suddenly there was a sharp tapping on the metal panel. "Hey, who's over there?" questioned the high-pitched singsong voice of a young male, probably no more than twenty-three years of age.

The faceless voice sent icy shivers up and down her spine and her gasp ended in a sob. An older, courser voice chuckled, "Ooh, we got us a scared sweet young thing, buddy. Too bad she's over there, or we'd be havin' us some fun for the next hour or so!" Grace felt like she was going to be sick. A burning taste of bile rose in her throat like an angry captive fighting to be free.

As the officer started the engine, she slid on the seat to the front of the van where there was a small panel window that she had noticed when she first stepped up into the van. It opened to the cab. Quickly she slid the panel to the side. What little light that came through only confirmed the suspicions of her nose that the inside of the van was filthy. It appeared that a previous passenger had used fecal material to write obscene comments on the inside panel of the van. There was also a dried white film spattered on both sides of the van, the floor, ceiling and some sections of the seat.

72

Panic was rising inside her like a volcano about to erupt. Leaning close in to the little window, she said as softly as she could, her voice shaking with emotion, "Please, I think I'm going to be sick. I can't ride like this."

The officer turned to look through the window at her, the smirk on his face belying the caring tone of his voice. "You'll be alright. There's a bucket strapped to the wall at the end of the bench by the door. If you feel you're going to puke, go down to that end and try to get it in the bucket. If you miss and make a mess you'll just have to ride in it for the next hour."

"Hey, darling," the younger voice called out again from the other side of the panel, "why don't you ask them to let you ride on this side with us? We can do things that'll take your mind off being sick." Both men broke out in laughter, and continued, taking turns, describing to her all the things they could do. She covered her ears with her hands trying to block out their words, as pictures filled her mind with each vivid description that was described to her. Suddenly, she was on her knees, head down in the bucket, vomiting.

Her vomiting was the catalyst that egged the men on in their crud and vulgar non-stop tormenting conversation. Sobbing hysterically, she tried to clean herself up with the few tissues she had in her pocket. She again begged the officer to help her. His cynical response hit her with the force of a hard fall, taking her breath away.

"Listen bitch, you need to sit back, shut the f…. up, and try to relax or we just may have to stop and put you in with the two men on the other side of the van. We'll be dropping them off at

73

the State prison before we take you to the State Hospital." She stared as the officer reached up and closed the sliding panel from inside the cab with a force that bespoke finality.

Now she was in total darkness again. It seemed to be closing in on her with a crushing force. The hooting and coarse conversation continued. In total disregard to the condition of the bench, she lay down and tried to cover her ears to muffle the sounds that penetrated the panel. "Ooh, baby, come on!" "Ooh, yea, that's it, here it comes!" The sound of splattering on the other side of the panel sent her again scrambling for the bucket.

Her hands were shaking so bad she could hardly get herself cleaned up again. She strained to keep her sobs from echoing back and forth in the van. Her mind reeled with shock from the graphic abuse that was coming through the panel like cold hard slaps in the face.

Her tormented soul cried out to God, *"I will never forgive Justin for allowing this to happen to me! God! Where are You? Why are You letting this happen to me?"* She slumped to the floor of the van, her head resting on the bench. Her mind spun back reluctantly in time to another haunting memory of her first exposure to a similar abuse that should have prepared her for what she was going through in the van but apparently had not.

This particular memory still made her sick to her stomach and could put her in a state of perpetual panic.

Justin had come home from work early, a very uncommon occurrence. She had been both surprised and delighted by his excitement and enthusiasm over his

74

discovery of a "new" store that he wanted her to go and check out with him. This was unheard of as he never wanted to go shopping with her. Her happiness over the unexpected adventure was tinged with apprehension as the drive took them to the Lower East Side of the city, known for its poverty, crime, and businesses of ill repute. She was not prepared for their final destination. . . . .

Justin drove to a part of town that Grace had never been to before.

"Where are we going, Justin?" she asked, a slight feeling of apprehension growing in the pit of her stomach.

Justin turned his head to look at her, a sly gleam causing his eyes to glisten darkly. "It's a surprise." he said and laughed out loud, throwing his head back.

The building was old, old and dirty. The bricks were rusty looking and stained. Where once large windows of a formally respectable storefront had displayed various items for sale, now painted clapboard, faded and chipping from the constant abuse of the weather and the residents of the neighborhood, hid unspeakable items. The single glass door was covered with heavy black paper on the inside. A neon sign flashed sporadically over the door, "ADULT VIDEO-BOOK-AND-PARAPHERNALIA." There were no trees by the building to provide shade from the constant on slot of the glaring sun, no gentle rustling of leaves giving way to a cooling breeze. The cracked uneven sidewalk was littered with cigarette butts in various lengths, and tiny flecks of the chipped white paint from the clapboard siding that rose like a dirty obscene sign above the bricks.

From across the street, you could just make out the heat waves rising from the cement against the black of the glass door. The closer you got to the building, the more aware you became of the strong stench of old cigarette butts mixed with urine that rose from the hot cement like a nauseating odor, riding on the back of the heat wave.

The surrounding buildings were similar in appearance, with dirty windows, broken sidewalks, and the swirling of litter and trash on the pavement.

On one side of the building was a parking lot. Justin pulled in and parked the car. Grace had to look at it closely to realize that there really was pavement underneath the swirling fluid sea of dirt, weeds, empty pop and beer cans, and broken glass liquor bottles, along with the ever-present cigarette butts, and crumpled brown fast-food bags. Along the wall of the building there were periodic spots where the brick had crumbled away and left gaping holes in eerie patterns. An overwhelming feeling of utter despair washed over her like a torrential rain as she reluctantly stepped from the car. Justin jumped out of the car in great excitement. *"Come on!"* he shouted impatiently, and grabbed her by the arm to steer her through the forbidding black door.

The hinges of the door whined with the need for a good oiling, and clashed with the sharp clang of the bell fastened to the top, heralding the arrival of another patron. A small fan hanging from the ceiling had absolutely no effect on the suffocating heat that hung in the air like a thick blanket. It did, however, manage to propel a nauseating mixture of smells around the crowded room. Everything from sweat and unwashed bodies, to alcohol, cigarette smoke, and the tangy aroma rising from the half eaten order of take-out Chinese sitting on the counter, seemed to permeate from every direction. A large burly looking man with slicked back greasy hair sitting on a stool behind the counter paused only for a fleeting moment to look up from his magazine as they entered the building. The other patrons did not show any sign of being aware that they had come in at all.

The room was full of racks that held videotapes, magazines and books. Hanging on the walls, on hooks, were packages containing every kind of "sex toy" imaginable. The suffocating stench combined with the shock of the items displayed was enough to give rise to the frantic desire exploding inside Grace to turn and run back out the door. That, however, was not an option since Justin gave her a push, and said, "Go pick out a magazine, honey. This is gonna be fun!"

Grace walked like a zombie over to the magazine racks and blindly picked up a magazine, flipped through the pages unseeing, and returning it to the rack picked up another. She had entered into a state of delayed shock, and was operating in self-preservation mode.

Justin, on the other hand, sauntered through the rows of videos and picked out a couple that aroused his interest, and then continued on over to the wall to check out all the "sex toys." After picking out one to his liking he came back over to her. "Find a magazine you want yet?" he asked, his voice hinting of sarcasm. Her dazed expression, as she stammered, "I. . . I

77

don't know, I. . . I can't find one." was enough to show him she was totally out-of-it.

"Here, let me pick one out for you." He picked out a magazine geared for women and then picked out a Playboy for himself. Sitting on the counter was an old fashioned cash register. He walked over to it and paid for his purchases. After talking to the sweaty greasy man, he hurried back to where she was still standing in a trance.

"Wow, this is so great. Come on, I want you to see something." He took her by the arm, his fingers like long icy cold steel claws, and pulled her through a door that was to the left of the counter. It led to a large room that was sectioned off with about ten small curtained booths. Each booth held a chair, a small screen and little projector that was operated by inserting quarters into a small slot on the side of the machine.

The air was stagnant and hot, heavy with the smell of sweaty bodies. Grace watched transfixed as he set his packages down on the dirt-encrusted floor that was strewn with cigarette butts and was sticky from spilt beer or pop. He dug in his pocket and pulled out a full roll of quarters. As he turned to look at her, his eyes gleamed with his pent-up excitement and anticipation. "Pay attention to that screen."

Grace's eyes were drawn against her will to a small spattered screen. She could hear the sharp clink, clink, clink of coins being inserted into the machine. Suddenly, a motion picture started playing across the screen. One sexual act after another was portrayed in poignant detail. Everything from one person masturbating, to couples in multiple positions, including oral sex was demonstrated. There were same-sex partners and multiple partners all interacting with each other; all of which paraded before her frightened innocent eyes. She had the horrifying feeling that the walls were moving toward her; the pungent smell of body fluids only added fuel to the already desperately intense burning feeling that she was suffocating.

Suddenly, she was aware of Justin positioning himself next to her. He opened the front of his pants. Grabbing her arm, he pulled her down to him, forcing her to kneel on the dirty, sticky floor almost in front of him. "Look at that!" he panted, his breath hot against her ear, "Do you see what they're doing? I want you to do that! Come on, do it now!"

He grabbed her hand and forced her take hold of him, and then he pushed her head down. When he was finished, she was on her hands and knees, choking and gagging. He leaned back in the chair spent from the exertion of the moment. "Oh god, that was awesome, baby. Didn't I tell you we were gonna have some fun?" His laugh was coarse and loud from his pent-up excitement. "Wait till we get back home. We are REALLY gonna have some fun then."

Grace again found herself vomiting into the bucket. She could still hear the voices on the other side of the panel, taunting and laughing. *God, where are You?*

Shaking with exhaustion from the vomiting and the shock of the constant verbal abuse, Grace slipped to a prone position on the floor of the van. With the ease of a tortured and beaten victim she gave herself to the engulfing darkness that settled over her like a deep soothing oblivion.

Chapter 8

Grace never knew how she ended up in the four-bed ward. Her suitcase and overnight bag were nowhere to be found. She sat up slowly, trying hard not to recall her last memory before passing out in the van. She shuddered as the taunting voices from the other side of the panel still played like a broken record in her head.

Slowly she slid her legs around to sit on the side of the bed. She grabbed hold of the bedside stand, trying to get her balance. Looking around, she could see she was in a fairly large room. There were windows along one wall that went from about three feet off the floor almost to the ceiling. There were no curtains on the windows, only a heavy iron-mesh covering. Each of the four beds had a nightstand and a small dresser close by. There were also four doors, that when opened, revealed a small closet containing hangers. Above the closet door was another door that opened to a storage compartment.

Grace carefully stood up, holding on to the bed until she was sure she would not fall. Her mouth was dry and she still felt very sluggish. Slowly, she walked to a door that she hoped led to a hallway. She turned the doorknob and opened the door, cautiously stepping out into the hall. Across the hall from where she stood was a door that was open revealing another room just like the one she had just come from. She could tell the room she was in was at the end of a fairly long hall.

There were two more rooms about ten to twelve feet down the hall. About ten more feet there was a large open room with a counter on one wall with an opening that revealed yet another room. There was a door to the left of the counter, which was the entrance into the smaller room behind the counter. Another five feet there was an open doorway with just a sign over the top that read "Bathroom."

Grace slowly walked down the hall, dragging her hand along the rough pitted cement wall as a point of contact and support. When she got close to the counter, she could see the big open room more clearly.

Two large couches were dwarfed by the size of the room. The worn and faded material was spotted with pop stains and black charred burn holes from cigarettes. Three women were slouched on one of the couches, each with a cigarette held between their fingers, watching a game show that was blaring from the television in the corner. A beautiful bouquet of red roses seemingly out of place stood in a vase on the stand beside the television. Their fragrant floral aroma was almost lost in the heavy pungent scent of the burning cigarettes and the thick blue haze that filled the air.

Rocking in one of the five rocking chairs that were sporadically placed about the room was a young girl. Her very skinny arms were tightly wrapped around a small worn teddy bear. There were a couple small groups of women sitting at several of the tables around the room. One group seemed to be working on a puzzle, heads bent, diligently trying different pieces of the puzzle on the unfinished areas. Every few seconds there would be a shout of triumph as another piece found its proper place in the puzzle. Another group was playing a card game, with gum and cigarettes being used for betting. An old upright piano at the far end of the room was emitting a slightly off key rendition of chopsticks being played by a woman who Grace was sure had to be at least fifty years old.

  On the far wall was a door that led out to a heavy iron-meshed type screen porch. There were also some battle worn bookcases running the width of the room, their shelves full of books, magazines, games, and movies on videotape.

  The noise from the television and piano along with the periodic shouts from the other patients was confusing and disorienting to Grace. She noticed three women and two men who seemed to be wearing some kind of uniform. Some were talking with the different groups of women and some were just standing around, like they were watching, waiting for something.

  Grace noticed a door labeled "Showers" the other side of the bathroom, and another just past that one that said "Laundry." A young woman with very short hair leaned against the doorframe of another four-bed ward. Her haunting eyes stared at Grace from across the room.

  "Grace?" At the sound of her name being spoken Grace jerked around to look into the face of a tall, broad shouldered woman in a nurse's uniform. She had coal black hair and a short stubby nose with black bushy eyebrows. Her voice was deep and gruff, like she had sustained an injury to her throat that she had not totally recovered from.

  "Yes?" Grace's voice trembled as she grasped the counter to keep from falling.

  "Grace, my name is Angela. I'm

the charge nurse for this unit. I have your things here with me. I've been marking them all with a permanent marker. Every personal item on the unit has to have the name of the owner on it. All your things are in this basket. You may take it to your room and put them away. When you're finished come back here and we will do your entrance interview. I will try to answer all your questions at that time." Angela paused as she bent over and lifted up a large green plastic basket and put it on the counter for Grace. She looked directly at Grace who was staring at her wide-eyed. "Did you understand what I just said?"

Grace swallowed hard, nodded her head, and reaching for the basket, grabbed a handle with each hand, and pulled it off the counter. She turned and walked back to her room. Once there, she placed the basket on the bed and stood staring at her things. Every article of her clothing had her name written on it in black permanent marker. Her photo album had her name on the back outside cover. Her shoes had her name on the inside sole. Her mother's Bible had her name on the inside cover page. Each of her journals had her name on the outside front cover. Her name was on everything. Tears streamed down her cheeks.

Even her underpants, bras, and socks had her name written on them. Grace acutely felt the loss of privacy and independence.

Carefully, she put her pajama's, socks and under garments in a drawer. She put her one extra pair of blue jeans in a drawer with the one sweatshirt and the four t-shirts she had brought, along with several pairs of shorts. She hung up her robe, two dresses, two skirts and blouses, and two pair of slacks in the closet.

In the bottom drawer of the dresser she put her photo album, journals, and her address book along with her stationary and stamps. She noticed her pen was missing and wondered if it was considered a weapon.

Grace put her sandals, tennis shoes and slippers on the floor in the closet. The basket was empty. She wondered where her toilet items were and headed back up to the nurses' station to find them.

Grace had to wait several minutes for Angela to get off the phone, and then she asked about her toilet items and her pen.

"We keep everyone's bathroom stuff in a little basket with your name on it up here. We hand out the baskets when you want to take a shower, or in the morning when you want to brush your teeth. If you need to shave your armpits or legs, someone will have to be with you. When you turn the basket back in, if anything is missing, we do a body and room search for the missing item. You may have your pen to write in your journal or write a letter, but you have to do it out here in the day room." Angela was walking toward the door, she turned her head to look at Grace, "Come around to the door on the other side of the counter and I will let you in and we can do your entrance interview and go over the rules."

Grace walked over to the door. She heard a click and pulled the door open. Angela took her to a small room and they sat down at a table across from each other. The next ten minutes were spent going over all of Grace's personal

85

information. The usual questions were asked; name, address, phone number, date of birth, the name and phone number of her nearest relative, her doctor's name and phone number, and verifying the list that had been made of her personal items. Grace noticed on the list that two cartons of cigarettes and a lighter were listed along with $50. Grace frowned. Looking up at Angela, she asked, "How did these get here?"

"Your husband had them with him." Angela was busy checking off her list and did not see the look of shocked sweep over Grace's face.

"My husband? Justin? He's here?" her voice cracked as her chair crashed to the floor. Angela looked up startled by the emotion radiating from Grace like a roaring fire in a fireplace. "No, he's not here now. He's already left. Said he had to get back to his office to prepare for a case or something he had this afternoon. He signed you in, left a few additional things for you, and then left." Angela continued writing on her list, but muttered under her breath. "I'd of thought he'd want to at least talk to you a minute before he left, since you can't receive or make any calls for the next fourteen days, but hey, it's none of my business."

"But, but, how did he get here? He wasn't in the van with me. Where was he? If he drove up, why couldn't I have rode with him? Does he know what Grace went through on the ride up here?" Grace stood, palms flat on the table, leaning across it toward Angela, her voice loud, bordering on hysteria. Before Angela could form a question to Grace's reference to herself in third person, the door behind Grace opened suddenly and two male staff members came

86

into the room. One came to stand on each side of Grace, quickly taking a firm hold of each of her arms.

"Need some help here, Angela?" the one on the left asked. Grace struggled to free herself. The pinching grip on her arms tightened to the point that she was beginning to feel pain. Hot tears formed wet trails that leaked down her cheeks and dripped from her chin as she suddenly sagged in defeat.

Angela watched as the two men put Grace back in her chair after setting it upright. Grace crossed her arms on the table, and dropping her head, sobbed uncontrollably. Angela looked up at the two men, and shaking her head, laid her pen down and reached over to touch Grace's arm. Both men left the room, but remained just outside the door.

"Grace, I know you came here under a court committal, and I also know that there were two men going to the state prison in the same van as you. I can only hazard a guess as to what you had to listen to on your way up here. There's no way your husband could have brought you, though, because the court committal. But, he also had to come because he had to sign all the paperwork. I'm sorry for what you had to go through, but I suggest you try to put it behind you so you can get on with the business of getting well. I want to help you, Grace, but you have to want to help yourself. Will you try?" Angela waited, watching to see how Grace would respond.

Grace did not lift her head. Through gritted teeth in a gruff, harsh voice she said, "Yes, I'm gonna try. I'm gonna more than try, but I will NEVER forgive Justin for doing this to Grace! Now…" Grace paused as she raised

her head to look at Angela, "…I really NEED a cigarette!"
Grace was never able to totally recall her first few days on the unit. The other women on the unit all had severe cases of mental illness, ranging from Paranoid Personality Disorder, Borderline Personality Disorder, Schizophrenia, Bi-Polar Disorder, to Anorexia, Bulimia and Binge Eating Disorders.
She did not see the specialist, Dr. Joseph Elgin, who was a specialized psychoanalyst in the field of Personality Disorders, until her third day on the unit. Grace had been so nervous about meeting with him, that she had actually lost her lunch, and had a hard time convincing Angela that she had not made herself throw-up.
When she did finally get to his office, the meeting was short, as her file had not yet arrived from Dr. Evans. He had asked her if she understood why she was there, and if she understood the diagnosis, Multiple Personality Disorder (MPD), and how someone got the disorder. Grace had stumbled around with her answers, stating she did not feel that she "had" multiple personalities, and that she was very anxious to work with him to disprove the diagnosis. He had looked up from his writing on a file over the top of his eyeglasses, hmphing to himself under his breath, and then had looked back down at the file, continuing his writing. He cleared his throat before continuing.
"Well, maybe we can clear up the confusion of all of this for you in our first real session, after I get your records from Dr. Evans. In the meantime, I want you to take a psychological test, called an MMPI, the

Minnesota Multiphasic Personality Inventory. It's a questionnaire that's composed of several hundred "yes or no" questions, with no real wrong answers. So don't spend a lot of time "thinking" about the answers. Just answer honestly. Any questions?" He had waited patiently for Grace to collect her thoughts.

Grace sat with her hands tightly clasped. She had thought of several things that she wanted to ask him before she arrived in his office, but now could not think of one of them. "I can't seem to remember any of the questions I had." She stammered, shifting uncomfortably on the chair. Suddenly Grace sat up straight and spoke in a calm, controlled voice, "I guess, for now, I just want to know if it will really take all of the ninety day committal to sort through this, or could I possibly be allowed to go home sooner? Also, how soon can I have a visitor?"

Dr. Elgin sighed, closing the folder on his desk. He removed his glasses and for a moment just looked at Grace. "I can't really answer that question, Mrs. Anderson. I have lots of patients, so I will probably only see you once a week. I have several psychology students from the university who work on my team. They will see you several times a week. We, along with the unit staff, will evaluate your progress and a decision as to how long you will actually be here will come from all of us, although, the final decision will be mine. Your cooperation and desire to get well will play a big part in my decision."

Dr. Elgin stood up and walked around the desk to her chair and took her by the arm. As they walked to the door of his office he continued, "The time will go fast if you don't dwell on it. Instead, concentrate on working through this. Depending on how you do your first fourteen days, I will probably have you moved to a different unit that is a little less traumatic, and then you can have visitors. I'll see you next Monday."

Grace was surprised to discover she was standing in the hallway, with the door closing softly behind her. Andrew, one of the male aides from her unit was sitting on the windowsill looking at a magazine. He looked up, grinning, "All ready then?" His voice sounded friendly enough, but Grace still found it difficult to not feel uneasy when in the presence of any man. She nodded without speaking. Smiling, Andrew put the magazine, rolled up, in his back pocket. "Ok, let's go. It's almost dinnertime. You're probably really hungry since you lost your lunch."

Grace did not answer, so the walk back to the unit was quiet and uneventful. Once back in the unit however, Grace watched in dismay as Andrew quickly left her to go and help Angela with Madeline, one of the women on the unit. She was standing close to the wall, methodically slamming her head against the wall, a red stain growing bigger with each impact.

It took both of them to wrestle her to the floor. Angela then forced her mouth open to pour a yellow liquid in, and quickly held it closed, forcing her to swallow. All the while she talked to her in a calm voice, telling her to not "listen" to the voices. It was several minutes before Madeline finally relaxed on the floor. A pillow

90

was placed under her head, and she rolled over on her side. Andrew sat cross-legged in front of her, as she was now tightly holding onto his hand. Angela carefully cleaned the oozing cut on her head and applied a bandage.

The three female aides were scattered about the day room, trying to calm the other women who were now completely wound up by the whole episode. Elizabeth, another young schizophrenic patient was yelling about the voices in the television telling her to take off her clothes. Phillip, the other male aide, was trying to keep her from following through on the orders. Jennie, a bipolar patient was digging at her arms. Susan, one of the female aides, was talking to her, trying to get her to stop.

Grace shook her head in confusion. The room was becoming too noisy with all the commotion and angry, agitated voices. She slowly slid down the wall to the floor, pulled her knees up tight to her body and rested her head on her knees. Covering her ears with her hands, she made an effort to shut out the frightening sounds. What seemed like only moments later, Grace lifted her head at the touch of a hand on her arm. She looked up startled into the face of Penny, another female aide.

"Are you finished with your dinner, Grace?" she asked, reaching for an empty carton of milk in the middle of the table.

"What?" Grace, asked, looking around, completely confused to now find she was sitting at one of the tables in the day room. Patty, one of the bulimia patients, sitting across the table from Grace, grinned through a mouth full of potato salad, and shouted out, "She's

b-aaa-ck!"
 Angela came walking over to the table. "Grace? How are you feeling? Will you take your medicine for me now?"
 Grace looked up at Angela. "What happened?" Her voice trembled with fear.
 Angela put a hand on Grace's shoulder in an effort to calm her. She pulled up a chair and sat down and looked into Grace's frightened eyes. "Grace, how much do you remember after you sat down on the floor in the hall?"
 Grace's face clouded over with bewilderment. She rubbed her forehead, trying to clear away the cobwebs of confusion. "I, I really don't remember anything after that except for Penny just now asking me if I was through eating my dinner. I don't even remember eating my dinner!" Grace's voice raised a level in volume and agitation.
 Angela slid the little paper cup that held Grace's pills in it toward her. "Don't worry about it, Grace. This has been a stressful day for you. Take your pills and if you want to we can talk some more about what happened."
 Grace sat staring at the pills. When she spoke her voice rose in volume, each word expressing her agitation and frustration. "What ARE all of these anyway? I really don't think I should be just taking these without knowing what I am taking and why!"
 Angela sighed. "Well, this little white one is an anti-depressant, and the green one is to help you relax. The yellow one is to help you not become constipated, as that is a side effect of the anti-depressant. The blue one will help you get a good night's rest. OK?"
 Grace knew she should not feel angry. She thought about how her parents had always cautioned her to not

"show" her anger as "people" were watching her, and more was expected of her than other people being in the ministry and all. Grace had hated that. It was not fair. She should behave and take the pills, but something inside her seemed to be raging to get free. Before she knew it, her hand flew out and the paper cup with the pills went flying across the floor.

Angela retrieved the cup and pills and came back to the table. She sat down in the chair and for a moment did not say anything. Grace felt panic rising up in her. "I'm sorry." she whispered, lowering her head in shame.

"Grace, can you tell me why you just did that?" Angela's voice was not condemning or angry.

Grace looked up, surprised at Angela's question. Why had she done that? "I don't know. I really don't know. I just feel so angry and I don't even know why!" tears of angry frustration coursed down her hollow cheeks, her voice now broken and childlike.

Angela reached out her hand and gently patted Grace's hand. "What's your name honey?"

Grace rubber her eyes hard, and looked Angela square in the eye. "My name's Grace Elizabeth Adams, but my daddy calls me Lizzy."

"I like that name. I have a best friend named Lizzy. And just how old are you, Lizzy?" Angela asked.

Lizzy's face broke into a big grin, "I'm nine and a half years old." she said.

Chapter 9

Grace woke the next morning more confused than ever. Her memory of the previous day was like a mixed up jigsaw puzzle, with several important pieces missing. What was really strange was she had a weird memory of feeling like she was outside her body watching herself at the table. Then knocking the pills to the floor and hearing herself talking to Angela – only it was not her talking, but a small child. A child who said she was nine and a half years old and was called Lizzy. Lizzy – which had actually been her dad's pet name for her.

Grace got up and dressed quickly. She wanted to talk to Angela to see if she could explain to her what had happened. As she opened the closet door to get her shoes she glanced around the room. The other girls were still in bed. It was not really dark out, but she could tell that it was early morning. Just how early she did not know.

Grace slipped out of the room and walked to the nurses' station. The clock on the wall over the desk said 6:05. She did not know when the shift change took place, and no one sitting behind the desk. She waited for several minutes, and then called out, "Is anyone here?"

A door off the nurses' station opened and Susan came out, closing the door behind her. "What's wrong Grace? Why are you up and dressed? It's not time to get up yet."

"I .. I'm sorry," Grace stammered, "I woke up startled and couldn't remember very well what had happened to me yesterday. I guess I'm just feeling confused and was hoping I could talk to Angela. Is she busy?"

Susan opened the door to the nurses' station and came out to Grace. "The night staff is giving her the report for their shift. If you're not sleepy why don't you go sit on the couch and I'll turn the television on for you and you can watch something. Everyone will be getting up soon. When we're through with report you can get your bathroom things and get cleaned up for breakfast and then maybe after breakfast Angela can talk to you." Susan had taken Grace's arm and guided her over to the couch. Grace reluctantly sat down while Susan turned on the television and then went back in to the nurses' station.

At 6:25 Grace got her stuff and went into the bathroom to wash up and brush her teeth and hair. After breakfast, Grace wandered the day room and hall waiting for Angela to be free to talk to her. She finally decided to go and get her journal and come back to the day room so she could write in it. When she got to her room, Dawn, another schizophrenic patient was lying on her bed. Grace decided not to try and deal with her herself and went to find some help. When she and Andrew got back to her room, Dawn was completely naked and was going to the bathroom on Grace's pillow.

It was a good hour before everything settled down again. Grace was given a whole new mattress, pillow and bedding. Susan helped her remake her bed. Grace struggled to keep from crying. How was she supposed to be able to concentrate on getting well with things like this happening all the time? Dawn was in restraints on a different

96

bed, and kept up a running conversation with the voices in her head, alternating between cursing and crying. At one point, Grace looked at Susan and asked, "Do I HAVE to stay in this room?"

Susan sighed, "We'll try to keep a closer eye on Dawn. She hasn't done anything like this in a long time. I will talk to Angela, though, and see what we can do."

After lunch, Grace wrote in her journal, played some cards with a couple of the other patients, and then spent three hours working on the MMPI psychological test. It wasn't until after supper that Angela finally came and got her and they went out to the porch area to talk.

At first Grace did not know what to say, but then she finally asked, "Angela, what happened yesterday? I have some really confusing and weird memories about it, and well, I have to say I'm a little concerned and even scared."

"What exactly do you remember about yesterday Grace?" Angela asked, looking down at the clipboard she was holding.

Grace was silent for a moment, thinking. Finally she recounted, "Well, I remember feeling very nervous about going to see Dr. Elgin, and losing my lunch. I remember seeing Dr. Elgin but then it gets fuzzy. One minute I was trying to answer his question, and the next I was out in the hall with Andrew. Then we came back here and there was a lot of commotion and ruckus going on and I remember starting to feel overwhelmed and sat down on the floor. Then I was at the table, and I had eaten my dinner, but couldn't remember eating it. Then you were talking to me, like this, and asking me how much I remembered of the afternoon's events. And that's the point when things get really strange."

Grace rubbed her forehead, and looked anxiously at Angela, "I have this foggy memory of feeling like I was outside of my body, watching me talk with you. It was me, but my voice sounded strange and I was acting in a way I would never act." Grace shook her head in frustration. "Does that make any sense to you?"

Angela was thoughtful for a moment before replying, "Well, Grace, sometimes a person can experience a feeling of detachment or even a sense of separation from their self. Reality can actually stay intact; you know what is happening, to a certain degree, but you don't feel like you're the one experiencing it. It's like it's happening to someone else." She watched Grace's reaction with interest. She could see confusion and panic starting to creep into Grace's face and countenance. "Grace? Do you understand any of what I just told you?"

Grace was silent for a moment then answered, "Yes, I think I do." Grace looked at Angela, fear and panic about to erupt from her like soda pop from a can that's been shook. "No. No, I don't think I do understand at all."

Angela reached out and gently took hold of Grace's tightly clasped hands. "OK. Let me try to explain it a little better for you. Sometimes, a person will have two or more distinct identities, each with its own unique way of relating to the world and to their self. Usually, at least two of these identities recurrently take control of the person's behavior. Frequently there is an inability of the person to recall important personal information to an extent that is more than ordinary forgetfulness. Some classic examples are finding new clothes in your closet which you don't remember buying, finding yourself in a place or situation and not being able to remember how you got there and having a complete loss of memory for what happened in the previous few hours to days to even weeks and months."

Grace's hands were dripping with sweat, an overwhelming desire rising up in her to run away. Angela could see the desire to run in her eyes, and held her hands tightly as she continued, "Grace, I don't think you have anything to be afraid of. I personally think that you may have experienced both of these things at varying degrees in your mind. I think the fact that you are starting to be more aware of this is going to help you to work through it. You're probably wondering why this is happening to you."

Grace nodded her head, staring at Angela, waiting for her explanation.

Angela was silent for a moment, trying to decide how far she should go with Grace on the subject. Finally, she smiled and said, "Grace, I think for now you should just know that what is happening to you is not something bad; neither does it mean that you have done anything wrong. The human mind is an amazing thing that we are still trying to understand. I don't want you to get all worked up over this. Why don't you write in your journal what you can remember and how you are feeling about all of it? I know that Dr. Elgin will want to talk to you about it. Can you do that for me, Grace?"

Grace didn't answer, but she nodded her head and slowly let her arms relax. Angela released her hold of

Grace's hands and stood up. "Do you write in your journal with a pen or a pencil?"

"A pen, please, and thank you Angela." Grace answered softly.

Angela headed for the doorway, and looked back at Grace. "Why don't you go get your journal and come back to a table here in the day room and I will bring you your pen so you can write a little more before going to bed?"

Grace again nodded her head and slowly rose to go to her room and get her journal. Her mind raced with all that Angela had just said to her. She knew that Angela was referring to multiple personalities. Did she really believe in such things? Was it really possible? She vaguely remembered watching a movie about a woman who supposedly had multiple personalities. She remembered how the movie had made her feel unsettled and she had had several nightmares after watching it. Was it possible that she really did have multiple personalities? Could it be that when situations arose that were too stressful for her that she just separated herself from the situation? Was she unable to deal with the situation? Maybe she just did not want to be responsible for how she did or did not deal with it.

Grace sat on the edge of her bed staring at her dresser. All her journals for the last twelve years were in the bottom drawer. She had never gone back through her journals to see what she had written. Why had she never done that? She did not know, but maybe she should. Grace got up slowly and opened the bottom drawer. She took the bottom journal, which was for 1977, the first year she had written in a journal, and then closed the drawer. She then grabbed her current journal and headed for the day room. Maybe she could sort some things out and be better prepared for her next meeting with Dr. Elgin. She really wanted to understand what was happening to her, and why. She wanted to get past it so she could go home. Home, home to what? More of what she had been living through for the last nine years? No, she could not; no she would not do that. Maybe she could get well enough so that she could be stronger and stand up to Justin. Let him know that she could not continue their marriage the way it had been.

But she was so scared. Could she stand up to him? What would she do if he would not change under any circumstances? For just a moment she was thankful that her parents were not here to see the awful mess she had made of her life and marriage. How disappointed they would be with her. Grace waited at the nurses' station for Angela to get her pen. Then she went and sat in a chair in the corner and opened her journal from the year 1977 and started reading.

It took Grace the next three days to read through the last twelve years of journals. She asked Angela for a yellow highlighter so she could highlight any writing that she did not recognize. By Thursday evening, her second full day of reading, Grace was becoming alarmed by how much of the journals she was highlighting.

Late Friday afternoon, Grace finished reading the last journal, which was for the current year. Grace sighed, setting the pink highlighter down, and rubbed her tired, burning eyes. She had only gotten a short way into the first journal when she realized that there were three different sets of handwriting. One was printing, like that of a very young child with many misspelled words. Another was a very neat script, with no miss spelling. The last was hers.

She had ended up with two highlighters, the pink for the childish handwriting and the yellow for the more neat script. Her own writing she did not highlight.

Grace picked up her journal and again read through her last entry.

Monday, June 26, 1989

I do not like this place. There are a lot of scary people here and I do not like the food. I wish I could go home to Pat. I think Justin is very mean to make us come here just cause he tired of Grace. He makes me so so so mad I could just hit him. He be sorry soon cause I am gonna tell on him to dr evans. She is nice to us. I am gonna talk to her next time I dont care what Elizabeth says. I can talk if I want to. I don't like taking all those pills. They make me feel funny sometimes. I wish pat would have brought my teddy bear. I like Andrew he nice to me and he funny but he better not touch me cause I'll kick him in the leg if he does. Angela says I have to go to sleep now. I miss mommy and daddy. I promised angela I would be good.

Good night.

lizzy

Grace reread the entry, frowning. She could not remember writing it, even in that, what had Angela called it, detached state of mind. It must have been that other one that Angela had talked about; the one where she just didn't have any memory of something for a certain amount of time. What was wrong with her? Why was this happening?

How long has this been happening and I wasn't even aware of it? These journals only go back 12 years and there

102

is so much writing in here that I do not remember writing! How long have I really been "losing time"? Since first grade? Since Tommy and Joe when I was five?

  Grace sat staring off into the past, not realizing that she was crying. Angela had been watching her closely for the last hour, and when she saw Grace look up from her journal and sit staring off into space, she walked over and carefully sat down beside Grace on the couch. Grace seemed oblivious to Angela's presence. Angela could see the last entry that Grace had been reading and could not begin to imagine what Grace must be thinking and feeling. Finally, Grace shook her head and looked back down at the journal. Her hands tightened their grip on the book and suddenly she flung it from her, sending it flying across the room.
  It landed hard on the floor sliding till it came to a stop up next to the piano. Grace covered her face with her hands and cried. Angela continued sitting beside Grace for a minute then got up and went over to the piano to retrieve the book. Grace was still sobbing when she sat back down next to her.
  Suddenly, a child like voice came from Grace's body. "She's so mad, Angela. She's so mad but she never, never, never lets it show. She always just keeps it inside. Sometimes I feel like we're going to explode!" Grace was rubbing hard at the tears running down her cheeks. As she turned to look at Angela, it was obvious that it was Lizzy talking. "Is she mad at me? She never gets mad or does anything wrong. It's always me that does that, but I'm just doing what she feels and won't do! Is

103

she mad at me for that?"

Lizzy fell into Angela's arms and continued to cry. Angela held her, patting her back and whispering soothing words to her. When Lizzy finally stopped crying, she sat up and wiped her face with the tissue that Angela gave her.

Angela leaned over to look Grace in the eye. "Lizzy, are you feeling a little better now?"

Lizzy raised her eyes to look at Angela. "Yes, I guess so."

"You threw the book didn't you? But it was Grace that wanted to, wasn't it?" Angela handed the book back to her.

"Yes." Lizzy answered barely above a whisper.

"Lizzy, do you know if you can "let" Grace know what is going on and let her hear what we are saying? Can you do that?" Angela asked in a quiet voice.

Lizzy looked at her wide-eyed. "I, I'm not sure. I can always feel her about to explode so I just take over and I guess most of the time she just kind a goes to sleep. But once in a while, I think she watches, but I don't know if she really knows what's going on. I think it's up to her."

Angela was thoughtful for a moment, and then she said, "Do you think you could try to let her hear me?"

Lizzy looked at Angela with large frightened eyes. "Am I in trouble Angela? Are you mad at me? Don't you want to talk to me anymore?"

Angela smiled, "Of course I'm going to talk to you, and no, you are not in trouble and I'm not mad at you. I am going to ask you to try real hard not to throw things. I know how bad you

would feel if something you threw hit someone else and hurt them. Can you try real hard not to throw things?"
"Lizzy smiled back at her. "OK. But sometimes we're so mad it's really hard not to throw things. Sometime we just want so bad to "hear" breaking glass that it's really hard not to do it."
Angela nodded her head. "I know. Sometimes, I get really frustrated, and want to punch something. You know what I do? I grab a pillow and just give it a good hard punch. Then I usually go and talk to my husband about it. So next time you feel like throwing something or you want to hear breaking glass, you go and punch your pillow, and then you can come and talk to me. OK?"
Lizzy smiled, her eyes shining, and she excitedly nodded her head.
"Now," Angela said, "do you think you could try and see if maybe both you and Grace could talk to me?"
Grace's eyes suddenly took on a glazed kind of look. Her hands came to her lap, and she clasped them tightly. Suddenly her eyes focused and she turned to look at Angela. She did not speak for a moment then she said in a calm, controlled voice, "I don't think this is a good idea, Angela. Grace is not ready for this. This is all too new and scary for her."
Angela raised one eyebrow and looked carefully at the very controlled Grace. "So, what's your name, dear?"
"I'm Elizabeth Adams, if you must know. This has been almost too much for Grace to deal with. She is pushing herself too hard I think. She really doesn't need to be here. I can take care of her. She really doesn't need your help or anyone else's for that

matter." Elizabeth calmly flicked a piece of lint off her slacks.

Angela sat quietly looking at Grace, who was now Elizabeth. When she spoke her voice was soft and calm, but firm. "Elizabeth, I know you care about Grace, and you think you can take care of her. But the fact is, Grace did try to kill herself and that's why she's here. If you really want to help her, you are going to have to work with her, and Lizzy and the staff, so we can help Grace to become a whole person."

"You want us to go away, don't you? You think Grace will be OK all by herself. But you don't know what it's really like. She is so tormented by all the garbage that has happened to her and by all the stupid stuff she's been told since she was just a little girl, that without us, she would already be dead. Is that what you want?" Elizabeth sat stiff backed, staring at Angela.

Angela sighed. "No, Elizabeth. That is not what I want, and no, I do not want you to go away. But she does need to be aware of things more than she is if she is ever going to be able to live a normal life. She can't keep losing time. That's a big part of her problem. She needs to learn how to cope, the way you do." Angela watched Elizabeth's face for some kind of acknowledgement of what she was saying. "If you really want to help her, you have to make her be more aware so she can learn to cope the way she should. She's just hiding now. She's not completely alive. She's only half, no, one-third alive. Do you understand what I'm trying to say?"

Elizabeth's hands were so tightly clasped that her knuckles were turning white. Finally her shoulders sagged and she lowered her eyes. "Alright, I will see what I can do. I can't make any promises. What Lizzy said is true. It really is up to Grace. But I will do what I can." Elizabeth looked up at Angela. "But you have to promise to keep Grace safe and to not let Justin hurt her ever again! Do you promise?"

Elizabeth's question puzzled Angela. Was there something about Grace's husband that she should know about? Angela was silent, searching for the right words. "Elizabeth, I can't make a promise that I don't know I will be able to keep. I can promise that while Grace is here with us, we will do everything in our power to keep her from being hurt. But really, whether Justin is able to hurt her again or not is also up to her. What I can promise you is, with your and Lizzy's help maybe we can help Grace to be able to do just that for herself. What do you say? Are you willing to try?"

Elizabeth was silent for a moment. Then slowly she nodded her head. "Yes, I will try." Suddenly, she was bouncing up and down on the couch. "I will too, I will too!" Lizzy's childish voice and laughter filled the room.

Angela smiled, nodding her head. "Good. Good."

Chapter 10

Friday, June 30th Grace went outside for the first time since she had arrived at Western State Hospital on the previous Saturday. It was a beautiful June day. The sun was shining, there was a soft, gentle breeze and the summer flowers were in full bloom. The wing of the hospital that Grace was in had a large fenced area. The patients could go there and feel safe and secure. Only one unit was allowed out at a time, so the amount of time wasn't long, but it was enough to be refreshing to the patients.

Grace wandered around, looking at the flowers and different shrubs. She looked out through the fence at the acres and acres of grounds and was awed by the majestic beauty of the view. The rolling acres of tall green grass, peppered with daisies and heather, swayed in the breeze like lovers in a gentle dance. And the trees! There were whole hillsides of them, their tall kingly tops reaching for the heavens.

Just before it was time to go back in, she watched a woman come out the door of the hospital and walk over to Angela. She bent over and spoke quickly to Angela, handing her a rather large brown envelope.

Grace wasn't close enough to hear what was said, but when she saw the look of alarm on Angela's face and then saw it turn from frustration to anger, she was surprised. Then, when Angela looked over and saw Grace watching her and then quickly turned away, Grace began to feel a twinge of apprehension.

After another fifteen minutes, Andrew, Philip, Susan and Penny began gathering everyone together to return to the unit. Grace waited in line to be inspected for any outdoor items that were not allowed on the unit.

   Once inside, Grace headed for her room but stopped short when Angela touched her on the arm and said, "Grace, may I talk to you for a minute?"

   Grace turned, and without a word, followed Angela into the same little room that she had had her entrance interview. Once inside, Angela spoke gently, "Sit down Grace. I have something to tell you and to give you."

   As Grace sat in the chair by the table, the door opened and Philip and Andrew came in and then closed the door, each standing with their backs to the door.

   Grace looked nervously toward Angela. "Have I done something wrong?" she asked in a frightened whisper.

   Angela sighed as she sat down. She looked at Grace, trying to determine "who" she was talking to. "No, Grace, YOU haven't done anything wrong." Angela noticed Grace's hands that had been laying flat on the table, come together in a tight clasp. Angela sighed again. Well, it was either Lizzy or Elizabeth, and she really wanted to talk to Grace. She thought for a second before she continued. "I really need to talk to YOU, Grace. Do you understand what I am trying to say?"

   Confusion filled Grace's eyes. Suddenly in a clear calm voice she spoke, "I don't think you have good news for Grace, so I'm not sure she should be here."

   "Elizabeth?"

   "Yes, Angela, it's me. What are you going to tell Grace? Is it bad news?" Elizabeth's face remained calm and unmoving.

110

"Well, it's not the best of news, but it's not the end of the world either. You can listen too, but I really need for Grace to hear this." Angela watched Elizabeth's face for any change.

"Can I listen too? Please, please, please!" Lizzy's childish voice begged.

"Yes, Lizzy, you may listen too, but you must promise me you will not get so angry that you throw anything or try to "hear" breaking glass. Can you promise me that?" Angela waited for Lizzy's response.

Grace's "Lizzy" face contorted to a childish pout and then a big sigh. "Oh all right. I'll try."

Grace's voice changed quickly and Elizabeth spoke, "She'll do more than just try. I will not let her act up. Now, I will let Grace come back, but I just want you to know that I can't always control her. So don't blame me if something bad happens."

Grace's face suddenly became blank, and she shook her head slightly. "I, I'm sorry, what did you just say?"

Angela laid the large brown envelope on the table and gently took hold of Grace's hands. "Grace, because you are here under a court committal, we are allowed to open your mail before you receive it. I need to tell you that this envelope is from a Mr. Jonathan Smith, one of the lawyers in your husband's firm. Your husband filed for divorce."

Grace caught her breath, her eyes large with shock, and suddenly pulled her hands free from Angela. She opened her mouth, but no words came out.

"I know this is a shock to you, but I want you to know that nothing can happen until you are released from here. You can make a call on Monday to hire an attorney to represent you, and I'm going to bend the rules and let you call your friend and housekeeper, Pat, tonight, if you would like to." Grace sat staring at Angela, still in shock. "Grace, did you hear me? Do you want to look at the paper work? I can look at it with you and try to answer any questions you may have."

Grace reached out and touched the envelope, but then jerked her hand back, as if she had been burnt. Finally she spoke, "I don't think I can look at it just now. Did you look at it carefully? Are you sure he's asking for a divorce?" Her voice broke with the last question.

"Yes, Grace. I read it through very carefully. He has filed for a divorce. I'm sorry." Angela glanced up at Andrew and Philip, shaking her head slightly.

Grace's face clouded over with a mixture of emotions. Tears fell silently from her eyes. She looked up at Angela and said softly, "Will you please keep this for me until I am able to look at it?"

"Of course, Grace. Would you like to go to your room and rest for a while?" Angela picked up the envelope as she stood.

"Yes, I think I would. I guess I really shouldn't be so shocked by this, but, well, you never know how you're going to feel when something like this is dumped on you." Grace stood and walked to the door. Andrew stepped aside and opened the door for her.

Angela looked at the frustrated frowns on the two faces of her aides. "I'm not real sure "who" just walked out of here. We need to keep her on a

112

suicide watch till further notice." Both nodded and left the room.

Darn. This did NOT need to happen right now. Angela went into her office to write on Grace's chart.

As Grace came through the door from the nurses' station and headed toward her room, Patty called out from a table where she and Madeline, Jennie and Elizabeth were playing cards, "Hey, Gracie, come play cards with us."

Grace didn't answer but kept walking toward her room. Andrew, who had followed Grace through the door, shook his head at the girls and followed Grace down the hall.

Philip walked over to the table. "What's wrong with Gracie now?" Jennie asked, holding up her cigarette for Philip to light.

Philip took a lighter from his pocket and lit her cigarette and then put it back in his pocket. "Don't worry about Grace. She'll be all right. So, who's winning?" Philip pulled up a chair and sat with them.

Andrew followed Grace to her room and watched from the door as she went and lay down on her bed. She turned on her side and closed her eyes. Andrew watched her for several minutes and then, noting the time on his watch, turned and walked down the hall to tell the other aides that Grace was on a suicide watch and to set up a fifteen-minute rotation between them all to keep an eye on her.

Grace lay with her eyes closed, but she wasn't going to sleep. She was trying desperately not to panic.

I can't believe he's really going to divorce me. What happened to us? What happened to him? Why did he change? He did love me once, and I think I loved him. Didn't I? How did this happen? What am I going to do? Oh God, I'm so glad daddy and momma aren't here to see this. They would be so ashamed. It's a good thing they're already dead 'cause this would for sure kill them. I wonder if there really is a heaven, can they see what's going on? Can they see me? I hope not! I'm such a failure. My whole life is just one big mistake and failure after another. Why couldn't I have just died? I really don't want to be here.

  Grace got up and paced the room. After fifteen minutes, Susan peeked in the room to check on her. Grace was still pacing. She stood just outside the door for a minute, and then went to find Angela.

  Angela was still writing on Grace's chart. She looked up when Susan came into the office.

  "What's up?" she asked, setting her pen down and closing the file.

  "I think Grace might need a little something extra to calm her down." Susan said.

  Angela stood up and walked out to the drug cart in the nurses' station. She opened the lower cabinet door with the key from her pocket and took out a bottle. She put one pill in a paper cup and handed it to Susan. "Take this with some water to Grace and see if you can get her to take it." She returned the bottle to the cabinet and relocked the door.

  Susan returned to Grace's room. Grace was still pacing. She stood in the doorway till Grace noticed her. "Grace, Angela would like you to take this pill. It will help you to relax." She waited, expecting Grace to refuse. Instead, Grace walked over and took the pill and popped it into her mouth, then took the paper cup filled with water. She opened her mouth for Susan to see that she had really taken the pill and then turned and walked back to the window.

Susan stood there for a minute. "Thank you Grace. Why don't you try and lie back down and rest for a few more minutes. OK?"

Grace did not turn around. "I'll try. Thanks for the pill."

Grace came down for dinner, but only pushed her food around on her plate. After dinner, Angela put a movie in for the women to watch, Superman. There was some arguing about the movie, but they finely settled down to watch it. Grace only lasted for ten minutes and then got up and headed down the hall to her room.

Angela followed her with her night meds, which Grace took without incident. When Angela left her, Grace was sitting on her bed in the dark.

Back in Seattle, Pat paced restlessly in her apartment. She felt an overwhelming burden for Grace. She glanced at the clock, 7:45 p.m. Suddenly the burden was so heavy that Pat dropped to her knees by the side of the couch and began to pray for Grace. She didn't know what could be wrong, but she felt a great urgency to pray, to intercede for Grace. She didn't stop until almost 9:00 p.m. when she finally felt a release.

Meanwhile, at the same time, up in Lakewood at the hospital, Grace continued to sit, staring at the closet door. Every fifteen minutes, one of the aides would come and check on her.

Grace felt like she was floating above her bed. She could see herself

115

sitting on the edge of the bed. She watched as Philip came to the door to check on her. He stood for a moment and then headed back down the hall. Grace watched herself stand up, go over to the dresser that was Dawn's and pick up two hospital gowns that had been laid there by Angela earlier.

    She watched herself tie the two gowns together and then tie the end of one gown around her neck. Then she watched herself walk over and pick up the heavy metal trashcan and turn it upside down in front of the closet. She then saw her self step up onto the can and reach up to open the storage cupboard door above the closet. She struggled to tie the other end of the gown around the hinge of the cupboard door.

    What is she doing? Am I dreaming? This must be just a dream.

    Grace watched herself pull hard on the gown to make sure it would hold and then with just a little effort, kick the trash can out from under her feet.

Chapter 11

Andrew was almost to Grace's room when he heard the trashcan tip over with a loud crash. He ran the last few steps to her door, yelling for help.

Philip, Angela and Susan raced down the hall, while Penny kept the other women distracted and Ann Marie dialed the inner-hospital 911 emergency help code. Within moments, the doors to the unit opened to admit three more female aides and three men. Ann Marie directed them to the room at the end of the hall.

Angela suddenly came out into the hall, calling for some shears. When Ann Marie reached the room, she was shocked to see four of the men supporting Grace while Philip, who was standing on top of the dresser, was trying desperately to untie the knotted gown. She handed the shears to Angela who handed them to Philip. In seconds he had cut the gown still tied to the cupboard door and they laid Grace on the bed. Angela carefully cut the gown from around Grace's neck, flinging it in the corner in frustration.

Angela's face was pale, and she fought for control of her emotions. She looked up at Susan who was brushing tears from her eyes. "There's a pulse, and she's breathing." Angela closed her eyes and shook her head in relief.

"She couldn't have been hanging there for more than 5 or 6 seconds." Andrew panted. "That's about how long it took me to get in here after I heard the trashcan fall."

Angela's voice was rough as she choked out, "I WANT EVERY ONE OF THESE DOORS REMOVED FROM ALL OF THESE STORAGE CUPBOARDS!" She turned and walked toward the door, then stopped and spoke without looking back at her staff. "Susan, stay with her, I'm going to call the doctor to come and check on her. Andrew, I want her in restraints!" Angela hurried out the door, but not before everyone heard a sob escape from her.

   Angela leaned back against the wall outside Grace's room taking deep breaths in an effort to calm herself. She had known she was walking a fine line with Grace. She brushed hard at the tears on her cheeks. Grace reminded her so much of her own daughter who had died only two short months ago. Mary Ann had been a couple of years younger than Grace, but she suffered from the same condition that Angela was sure Grace had. She had been devastated to learn that a neighbor man, who had died long before Mary Ann had ever talked about what happened, had molested her precious Mary Ann as a young child.

   She had not been able to save Mary Ann. Her throat was still mending from where Mary Ann had hit her just before she had scrambled over the railing on their balcony and plunged to her death.

   Angela straightened her shoulders and hurried down the hall to the nurse's station to call Doctor Abernathy; he was on call tonight. She would have him come in and check Grace. SHE WAS NOT GOING TO LOSE GRACE!

   Angela wrote the time on Grace's chart as she dialed Dr. Abernathy's number, 9:00 p.m. How could this have happened? Suddenly Doctor Abernathy answered his phone.

   Angela quickly related the incident and Doctor Abernathy said he would come right over to check on her.

   Angela looked up as Philip came up

to the counter. "She's awake. You'd better come."

When Angela came into the room she found Grace struggling against the restraints. Susan was trying to calm her, as Andrew and three of the other men tried to hold her still. She was jerking hard on the restraints and they were concerned she was going to injure herself further. Angela could see the bright red welt around her neck. Grace's face was a kaleidoscope of emotions. Her eyes showed pure panic.

Angela came close to the bed and bent over, gently brushing strands of damp hair out of her eyes. "Grace, can you hear me? It's Angela. Grace, can you try to relax a minute and talk to me?"

Grace's head stopped turning back and forth on the pillow and she looked directly at Angela. Her voice was hoarse sounding from the injury she had sustained from the tight gown about her neck. "I told you I couldn't always control her! I told you! THIS IS NOT MY FAULT!"

Suddenly Grace started crying. Her bottom lip quivered. Her eyes were large and frightened. "Angela, my froat hurts! It hurts real bad! It hurts to swallow."

Angela leaned forward gently stroking Grace's forehead. Softly she whispered, "It's going to be OK Lizzy. I'll get some ice, which should help the pain." She straightened up and glanced at Philip, who nodded his head and headed for the ice machine in the office. "Elizabeth, I don't blame you for this. It's not your fault. You are all going to be OK. We'll get through this, together. Dr. Abernathy is on his way and once he checks you we'll try to

make you more comfortable. OK?"
     Grace's lip continued to quiver as she continued to cry softly, but nodded her head, no longer thrashing about.
     Angela looked at Andrew and the other men and said she thought they could handle the situation from here on and thanked them for coming so quickly.
     Dr. Abernathy arrived after about twenty minutes and took several minutes checking Grace to be sure she was OK. He ordered X-rays and said he thought that maybe an MRI should be done also. He wrote an order for some cream for Grace's neck and a neck collar for her to wear. He did not want her getting up until the collar had been put on her. She seemed to have a very slight weakness on the left side, which made him decide positively to have the MRI done the next day.
     The neck collar was brought in before Dr. Abernathy was ready to leave so he put it on her after applying some cream and a bandage to the red welt area of her neck.
     After promising to return to talk to her, Angela left Grace with Susan sitting at the side of the bed and walked to the office with Dr. Abernathy.
     "I really think she should remain in restraints at least for the rest of the evening." Dr. Abernathy said as he reached for Grace's chart and began filling out his injury report.
     Angela sighed, knowing the ordeal she would have to go through when she informed Grace that she would be spending the night in the restraints. She also knew that Dr. Abernathy was right, and she did not want to take any more chances with Grace either.
     When Dr. Abernathy finished his report, he turned back several pages to

read through Angela's notes on Grace, from her entrance interview, to Grace's reaction to receiving divorce papers. When he had finished reading the notes through twice, he looked up at Angela with some concern.

"Angela, are you sure you are up to this? Isn't this a little too close for you? I'm sure that Grace could be moved to another unit without too much difficulty. She's not been here that long for it to make too much difference."

Angela folded her arms in front of her and firmly shook her head no. "I think this case is JUST what I need! I think in working with Grace to help her work her way through this, I will actually be helping myself, too." Angela leaned forward and looked directly into Dr. Abernathy's eyes. "I need this, Albert, please trust me. I know I can help this woman."

Dr. Abernathy sat silently looking at Angela, his eyes never leaving her face. Angela met his gaze, refusing to look away. Finally Dr. Abernathy heaved a sigh, and shook his head slightly. "All right, but I better not hear that you are having ANY chest pain, and I want you to get at least eight hours of sleep a night. Are you eating? Are you still having trouble sleeping?"

Angela smiled. "I'm fine, Albert, really. I'm sleeping better, and yes, I am eating. Every day is a little better than the previous one. I'm fine, really."

Dr. Abernathy stood up handing the chart to her, and picked up his black bag. Angela walked him to the unit door. He paused at the door to look at her. "I see something in your eye, Angela. Be careful, OK?"

Angela put her hand on his arm, nodding her head. "I will. Don't worry."

Penny and Ann Marie were still in the day room with the other women. The movie was almost over, and they were going to get them ready to receive their bedtime meds. Angela went to the medication cart and began setting up the medication. Thirty minutes later the movie ended and Angela handed out the medications. The aides made sure all the medication was taken, then worked with the women to get them ready for bed; handing out their bathroom totes, towels and washcloths.

It was close to 10:45 before Angela was able to make it back down to Grace's room. She only had a few minutes before she had to get ready to give report to the night shift. She had really wanted more time than that, but getting the meds passed out always took a long time.

When she entered Grace's room Susan looked up, relief evident on her face. Angela nodded at her and Susan turned to Grace as she stood. "I'll see you in the morning, Grace. I hope you have a good night."

Angela came over to the side of the bed and looked down at Grace. Grace was laying on her back, both arms and legs in restraints, her eyes shut. Angela could tell, just by looking at her, that she was uncomfortable and in pain. She sighed softly and sat down in the chair that Susan had vacated.

She reached out and gently touched Grace's hand. "Grace?"

Grace turned her head away and did not answer. Angela was silent for a moment, then patting her hand, slid the chair back and stood to leave.

"Please don't leave." Grace whispered, her eyes still tightly shut.

Angela was silent for a moment, then pulled the chair back up to the bed and sat. "I only have a few minutes before I have to go and give report to the night shift, Grace. Do you want to talk to me now, or do you want to wait till morning?"

Grace's eyes flew open and she turned her head quickly, groaning from the pain the movement caused, to look at Angela. "Aren't you going to take these restraints off?" Her voice was a mixture of panic and frustration, her hands clenching into fists and then unclenching repeatedly.

"I'm sorry, Elizabeth? I can't do that. Dr. Abernathy wants the restraints on until at least tomorrow morning. What happened to you tonight was a very serious thing. You could have died." Angela paused in an effort to gain control of her emotions. "Do you really want to die, Grace?"

Grace's hands suddenly went limp, she closed her eyes, but the tears came anyway. Her body shook with the sobs that rose from her crushed and broken spirit. Angela reached over and took hold of one of the limp hands. Grace's grip tightened as she continued to cry. Angela waited patiently. Finally Graces was able to stop crying. Angela wiped her face with a tissue, and Grace slowly turned her head to look at Angela.

"Did I really try to hang myself? It wasn't just another bad dream?" Her voice shook with emotion. "I thought I was just dreaming, although I guess I did really want to die. I'm so scared and ashamed. I really don't deserve to live."

Angela looked into Grace's sad,

troubled eyes. "Grace, it's really not your decision to make if you "deserve" to live or die. That's God's decision, and if my memory serves me correctly, we all *deserve* to die, but someone died in our place so we wouldn't have to."

Grace continued to look at Angela, and then said very slowly, "He may have died for you, but He didn't die for me. I've done too many terrible things for God to ever be able to look at me and say I am forgiven."

Angela's left eyebrow rose as she pulled her head back slightly and tipping her head to the right she asked, "Are you *limiting God?* Are you putting a *restriction* on whom and how much He can forgive? Just how do you figure you have the right to do that?"

Dismay and wonder flashed across Grace's face. Angela leaned forward, and said in a gentle, yet strong voice, "Titus 3:5 and 6 says: *'Not by works of righteousness which we have done, but according to His mercy He saved us, by the washing of regeneration, and the renewing of the Holy Ghost, which He shed on us abundantly through Jesus Christ our Saviour.'** That doesn't sound to me like you can decide who and how much He can forgive. Sounds to me like it's His decision."

Grace opened her mouth, but then closed it. Tears flowed from her eyes and streamed down her cheeks. Angela smiled gently. "He loves you, Grace, even if you don't love yourself or can't see or understand how He can. It's such a wonderful gift. Don't throw it away." Angela stood up to leave, and turned at the door. "Think about what I said. Try to get some rest and we'll talk again tomorrow."

Titus 3:5-6; King James (Authorized) Version

Grace lay there in the dark, tears on her cheeks. *Could He still love me, even after all I have done?*

Chapter 12

Grace had a restless night. She kept waking from frightening and disturbing nightmares. When she woke at 3:40 a.m., Grace was alarmed to discover the "dream" she was having was actually real. Dawn was standing over her with a pillow. Grace managed to scream before Dawn lowered the pillow unto her face. Still being in restraints Grace had no way of getting the pillow off her face. Just before she passed out she heard a muffled shout.

When Grace opened her eyes, she was no longer in restraints. At first she was confused, but then she realized she was lying on a bed in the small room off the nurses' station. Besides the bed, there was a desk in the room and an easy chair. A small bookshelf in the corner was covered with books. The bedside table held a small lamp and clock radio. The time on the clock displayed 4:15 a.m. Grace noticed a Bible on the table. *Whose room is this?*

The door to the room was open to the nurses' station and Grace could see a woman standing at the counter. As she turned toward the door to the small room Grace quickly closed her eyes and pretended to be asleep.

The radio on the bedside table was playing very softly. Grace strained to hear the music. She felt like it had been forever since she had listened to a radio.

What was she doing in here any way? How long had she been here? Suddenly, she remembered Dawn lowering the pillow on her face and not being able to breathe. Well, someone must have heard her scream and got in there in time, since she was obviously not dead.

Why do these things keep happening to me? Angela said God loves me, well, where is He? If He loves me so much, why do these things keep on happening? Maybe He's punishing me for trying to kill myself. Have I committed the "unpardonable" sin? Am I doomed to go through the rest of my life alone, by myself, and not even be able to "feel" God? Always wondering if He has really forgiven me? Never knowing for sure if I am going to heaven or hell? Why do I even think I should expect to know if God would forgive me or not? Why do I think I even deserve anything? This really is hopeless. I should have just kept quiet and let Dawn smother me.

Grace turned on her side, salty tears burning her eyes and stinging her cheeks. She put her hand over her mouth in an effort to keep from sobbing out loud. As she lay there on the bed trying not to think very slowly the voice on the radio penetrated her mind.

"This is Rick on WLCQ, the Voice of Hope, coming to you in these blessed sweet hours of the morning. If for some reason you are finding it difficult to sleep, then sit with me for a while as we listen to the encouraging words from this awesome song by Kevin Shorey. For that someone out there who right now is struggling to keep holding on, I pray the words of this song will bring you hope and give you the strength to <u>"Keep Holding On"</u>.

"You're surrounded by the night,
you've lost your will to fight,
there's no way out so it seems.
Ya say there's no hope,
you're at the end of your rope,

your life is nothin' but shattered dreams.
If mistakes run your life,
the guilt cuts like a knife,
let me tell you what my God can do.
(my God can do)
No matter the problem,
I know Jesus He can solve them,
so hang on and He'll see you through.

Keep holdin' on, He's right beside you.
Keep bein' strong,
He'll be there to guide you.
If you should fall, don't end it all,
keep holdin' on.

You're feeling all alone,
you say from here, where do I go?
I know someone who'll make your life new
oh yes He will..
You say you want to die,
first give this a try,
call out, JESUS, and He'll come to you.

Keep holdin' on, yah keep holdin' on,
He's right beside you,
He's right there with you.
Keep bein' strong,
He'll be there to guide you.
And if you should fall, don't end it all,
Keep holdin' on.
Just keep holdin' on to Jesus,
He's right beside you,
He's right there with you.
Ya gotta keep bein' strong,
He'll be there to guide you.
And if you should fall,

please don't end it all,
Keep (just)
Keep (just keep)
Keep (just keep holdin')
Keep (just keep holdin' on)
Keep holdin' on."*

    Grace lay alone in the darkened room, with only the dimmed night light of the nurses' station filtering through the partially open door. Her heart pounded like a hammer in her ears as the words to the song worked their way into her troubled, broken heart and spirit. She lay there trembling with the realization that she had not heard that song just by chance. She knew, beyond a shadow of a doubt, God was reaching out to her. Reaching out to her, Grace – to her, the rebellious, angry, hurt Grace who was so filled with anger at all that had happened to her that she couldn't deal with any of it any more.

    "God," Grace whispered, "is this You trying to tell me something? Are You trying to tell me that You will be here with me, and if, no, I should say, when I fall again, You will still be here, to help me get back up and keep holding on?"

    Grace could not see anyone else in the room, but she felt like someone was there with her. She sat up slowly, straining her eyes in the darkness, trying to see if someone was there. "Hello is someone there?" she whispered. Her eyes searched the room as her arms tingled and the hairs stood up. No one answered, because no one was there. Yet, she felt like she was not alone. Grace lay back down, pulling the blanket up under her chin. She lay there

*Keep Holding On Words & music by David Elchler & Kevin Shorey listening to the silence in the dark, the radio now so soft she could not make out what was being said. Grace felt herself slowly relaxing, almost as if she was drifting on a cloud. She felt a rush of fresh tears spilling down her cheeks, but she also felt a smile on her lips.

"Jesus?" Grace whispered, "Jesus, the guy in the song said I could just call out to You, and You would come to me. If that's true, Jesus, I'm calling out to You. I'm calling out to You!"

Grace's eyes shut as fatigue finally won the battle. But just before she drifted off to sleep, Grace felt a hand rest softly on her cheek, and fingers gently wipe the tears away.

Grace woke from a sound sleep to Angela sitting on the side of the bed, her hand resting on her shoulder. "Grace? How do you feel this morning?"

Grace sat up, her eyes large with wonder and excitement. "Angela, do you know WHAT happened this morning?"

Angela sighed. "Yes Grace, I do. I'm so sorry. Dawn is being moved to another unit. That must have been terrifying for you. Are you OK now? How does your throat feel?"

Grace put her hand up to the white foam collar. She had almost forgotten about it. Her eyes were still huge with wonder and excitement. "No, no, I don't mean that, what happened with Dawn, I mean what happened in here. When I woke up in here! Do you know what happened?"

Angela was surprised by Grace's attitude, and wondered who was really talking to her. What could have happened to get her all excited? "No, I guess I don't know what happened. Why don't you tell me?"

Grace sat cross-legged on the bed,

her eyes bright with excitement and wonder. She quickly related to Angela how she woke up in the room, confused, and then had cried feeling depressed and alone, but then she heard the song on the radio. She was silent for a moment, concentrating, and then she quoted word for word the song she had heard. When she was finished, she told how she had done what the guy in the song had said to do. She had called out to Jesus. For a moment her eyes lost their focus, and she seemed to be looking back to the last few hours. A peaceful smile touched her lips.

"As I was falling asleep I felt a hand gently wipe my tears away. Angela, do you think that was Jesus?" Grace now looked at Angela, her eyes searching her face for the truth.

Angela had sat on the side of the bed staring in wonder at Grace, feeling like a wind was rushing through her. Now she saw in Grace's eyes the question, *"Did this really happen or is it another one of my fantasies?"*

Angela only paused for a moment before she answered.

"Grace, I don't believe this was a fantasy." She reached out taking hold of both of Grace's hands, giving them a gentle squeeze. "Grace, you have been blessed with a very special encounter with the one person you can always depend on, the one person who will NEVER leave you or forsake you. Don't ever let this experience fade away. Hold on tight to it. Never ever let go of it. He keeps His Word, Grace. You can always trust that."

Grace's eyes, still large with the wonder of it all, were filling with tears, but there was a smile of hope on her face.

132

Just before breakfast Grace went for her MRI. When she got back, she had a bagel and some juice that Angela had saved for her. She then was allowed to call Pat.

When Pat answered the phone, she was so surprised to hear Grace's voice. She immediately started firing questions at her before Grace could even give her the news about the divorce papers.

"Grace, dear, I'm so glad you called. I had a terrible night last night. I was so burdened for you. I think it was around 7:45 that I had to just get down on my knees and pray for you. It was so intense, that I kept praying till about 9:00, when suddenly it seemed to lift and I was able to rest. But I still tossed and turned in bed, praying for you every time I woke, till about 4:30 this morning, when I finally fell asleep again and really slept soundly. So how are you dear? I can't believe they let you call. I thought you weren't allowed to make any calls for fourteen days? What's up?" As Pat paused for breath, Grace almost laughed because she was sure Pat had just said everything on one breath of air.

"I'm OK Pat. Angela, the day shift charge nurse is making an exception and letting me call you because I was served divorce papers from Justin yesterday." For just a moment Grace's voice broke.

Pat couldn't cover her mouth fast enough to keep Grace from hearing her gasp. Then she quickly spoke, "Oh, honey, I'm so sorry. Is there anything I can do?"

Grace was silent for a moment, thinking about what Pat had first told her, and then she spoke softly. "You

133

have already done something for me Pat, and you didn't even know it." Grace paused for a moment again to try and gain control of her emotions. "Pat, I have to tell you something that I'm ashamed of, but I really need to tell you."

Pat listened in stunned silence as Grace related the past evening's events as best she could remember them, from watching herself hang herself to hearing the song on the radio and calling out to Jesus. The entire time Grace could hear Pat intermittently crying and whispering softly, "Thank You Jesus – thank You for Your mercy and grace. Thank you for keeping my girl safe and making yourself so real to her!"

Grace began to cry. "Pat, I've been so awful, so angry, so rebellious. I hurt and disappointed my parents while they were still alive, and I know that I have hurt you, too. Can you forgive me? I'm going to need your love and support now more than ever!"

Grace continued to cry softly as Pat spoke loving encouragement to her, reassuring her that there was NOTHING she could ever do to make her stop loving and caring for her. They talked for over a half and hour, and when Grace said good-by, she was able to relax knowing that Pat would begin at once to get a lawyer lined up for her, and to see about getting the rest of her personal things from the house.

When Grace hung up the phone, she turned toward Angela. She stood there for a moment, clasping and unclasping her hands. Angela waited for her to speak. Finally Grace straightened her back and looked directly at Angela and spoke. "Thank you, Angela, for letting Grace telephone Pat. She really needed to talk to her." Grace was Elizabeth again. Elizabeth paused for a moment, and then continued. "She seems to be handling things pretty good doesn't she? I almost feel like I'm not needed anymore."

Angela watched Grace for a moment, and then spoke to Elizabeth. "How does that make you feel, Elizabeth?"

Elizabeth's voice was a little shaky. "Well how do you think it makes me feel? I've been dealing with all this crap for her for a long time and now all of sudden she thinks she can do it alone? Well, she can think again, I'm not going away. I've kept her out of a lot of messes when all she could do was "shut down" and then little miss naughty, Lizzy, was always jumping in and getting her in trouble. But am I appreciated? Noooooooooo! It's NOT FAIR!"

Angela looked at Andrew who had just come quietly through the door and shook her head. She felt confident she could get Elizabeth under control without his help.

Angela watched as Elizabeth struggled to regain her normal controlled demeanor. She swallowed several times as her emotions fought for control. Angela could tell she was losing the battle. Suddenly Elizabeth's hands went limp and her head dropped. Slowly her head came up and a frightened, tearful voice said, "Angela, does Grace want me to leave, too? Do I have to go away? If I promise to be good, if I promise not to break anything any more, do you think she would let me stay? Do you think she hates me? If I say sorry, do you think she'll forgive me? Will you ask her for me? Please?"

Tears, like an open faucet, were

now flowing down Grace's face, and she rubbed her eyes hard trying to stop the flood, sniffing loudly.

    Angela reached over and patted Grace's hand, knowing she was now with Lizzy. "Lizzy, neither you nor Elizabeth have to worry about Grace wanting to make you leave. She doesn't even really know you yet, and actually, you really ARE her, just a different part of her. She can't really send part of herself away now, can she?"

    Lizzy's eyes became large with amazement. "That's right! She can't send us away 'cause we're really part of her! She's so sad and scared all the time. She'd never have any fun without me. And, I'm the one who always has to put up with all the bad stuff that happens. What would she do without me?"

    Angela smiled, "I don't think she could make it without you! And, I don't think you could make it without her or Elizabeth."

    Lizzy frowned. "Elizabeth doesn't always like me. She gets mad at me when I get mad and break things." Lizzy suddenly looked up and mischievously giggled. "She likes people to think she never gets mad, but she does. She just holds it all in. She's so C-O-N-T-R-O-L-L-E-D! But I know what she does when she's about to pop." Lizzy suddenly covered her mouth, and her eyes became large and frightened.

    Angela reached out and gently took her hand. "What does she do, Lizzy?"

    Lizzy chewed her lower lip, rocking nervously in the chair. Suddenly she whispered, "She hides, too. She just goes away and if I don't come then poor Grace suddenly finds herself in a strange situation. She feels like she's going crazy. She has a lot of strange feelings and she's mad and hurt. She doesn't know what to do or even what's going on. When she can't figure it out, she becomes even more upset. Sometime I can't help her and then she does stuff that she's ashamed of and then she goes away too and I have to try and fix everything." Lizzy was crying and did not even know it. "Does that seem right, Angela? I mean, I'm only nine and a half, why should I always have to take the blame for everything?"

Angela glanced over at the tape recorder that she had started when Grace had hung up the phone. Dr. Elgin was going to want to listen to this one. Angela took a deep breath. "No Lizzy, it doesn't seem fair. That's why you need to talk to Dr. Elgin when Grace goes to her appointment on Monday. Both you and Elizabeth need to talk to him and if somehow Grace could be there too, listening, I really think it would help her. It should help Elizabeth too, and you, for that matter. If you can all understand how each other feels, and what a wonderful part of the whole each of you is, you will all just get better and better."

Grace sat up straight, brushing the hair out of her eyes. She folded her hands and looked at Angela. Elizabeth was back. "Do you really think that will work? Do you really think we can work together to be "one?"

Angela knew how she answered Elizabeth was very important. She licked her dry lips and answered very slowly and firmly. "Elizabeth, I believe that with all my heart. I know that the three of you can learn to accept each other's differences, strengths and weaknesses. You each have different talents and abilities, and

137

yes, different weak points. You can learn to help each other. You can become a whole person, with different facets, different characteristics, but you can be three people in one." Elizabeth sat quietly studying Angela's face as she asked, "Do you understand what I am saying to you?"

The look on Elizabeth's face seemed to change before Angela's eyes, almost a fluid movement. She could see Elizabeth's calm, controlled eyes and lips firm up as she nodded her head, but she also saw the childish longing and frightened eyes as Lizzy began to chew her lip and nod her head at the same time. But it was the slightly confused, almost dazed look in Grace's eyes as she shook her head slightly and opened her mouth to speak that made Angela realize they had just hit a milestone in Grace's journey.

"Angela? I feel really strange. I could hear myself talking, but it didn't feel like I was talking. What was happening? Am I OK? Am I going crazy?" Grace was back and trembling with exhaustion.

Angela smiled. "You're not crazy, Grace. You're just getting well."

After lunch, Grace sat at a table in the day room and tried to write in her journal. Angela watched from the counter of the nurses' station, apprehension slowly eating away at her hopeful feelings about Grace. She silently prayed for guidance as she struggled with the growing fear that maybe she had moved too fast. She was planning on listening to the tape of her time with Grace and then documenting it all in her chart. She had hoped Dr. Elgin wasn't going to feel she had moved too fast, but she was having second thoughts now herself.

Angela sighed as she stood up and headed for the door. Grace seemed to have been arguing with herself about something in the journal and had finally tipped over the chair, throwing the journal and pencil across the room. Andrew was by her side even before Angela got the door open. She watched with amused curiosity as he appealed first to Elizabeth, and then to Lizzy to stop fighting and not to do anything more that would cause Grace further humiliation. His words seemed to put a momentary stop to their destructive behavior. After picking up the journal and pencil, Andrew sat down on the couch. Angela thought it had to be Elizabeth on his right.

With her back straight, sitting on the edge of the couch, she talked in a controlled manor, her clasped hands in her lap. After a minute of talking, she suddenly jumped up and then she was "Lizzy", on Andrew's left side, sitting cross-legged, waving her arms in the air. Andrew almost looked funny as his head kept turning to follow her back and forth movement. Angela glanced around the room; thankful that no one else seemed to be paying much attention to the discussion that was taking place.

As she finally approached the strange little scene, Andrew looked up, his eyes twinkling with amusement, as he suddenly said, "Ladies, ladies, I think Angela would like to talk to Grace a moment, if you two could kindly put off resolving this little issue for a moment."

Lizzy stopped bouncing on the couch and looked up at Angela, "Did you hear him? He called me a "ladies." I'm a "ladies" - that's good, isn't it?"

Angela could not help but laugh as she dropped down on the couch next to Lizzy and gave her a hug. "Yes, Lizzy, that's good."

Elizabeth stiffened for a moment with Angela's arms around her, and she said in a forced voice, "Lady my ass. She's a spoiled, self-centered brat!"

Lizzy almost knocked Angela off the couch in her struggle to get free. "I am not spoiled!" She roared in indignation. "And I am not that other thing you said either. You're a meanie 'cause you always got to have things your way." She crossed her arms and slouched down in the couch, pouting.

Angela looked at Andrew, trying desperately not to start laughing, imploring him with her eyes to say something. Andrew cleared his throat and turned to look at Lizzy. "Lizzy, of course you are not spoiled or self-centered. But you have to try a little harder not to throw things. I thought you promised Angela you wouldn't do that anymore?"

Lizzy seemed to cave under his gentle rebuke. She raised her big blue eyes that were now filling with tears to look up into his kind but slightly bemused face. "I'm sorry, Andy. Do you not like me any more?"

Andrew grinned at her reference to "Andy" and gently wiped a tear from her cheek. "Of course I still like you. Will you promise to try harder not to throw things?"

A grin burst across her face as she rubbed her nose with the back of her hand. Before she could reply her posture changed and she frowned at Andrew. "You're patronizing her. She's never going to change if you keep this up. I thought we were supposed to be

140

helping Grace."

Angela now gently touched Elizabeth's tightly clasped hands, "Elizabeth, we are trying to help Grace. You and Lizzy are both a part of Grace. True, a part she doesn't know very much about, or really can't understand right now, but still a very real part of her. She needs both of you and your unique characteristics and abilities to become a whole person."

Elizabeth looked long and hard at Angela, measuring her words against the kind caring face she could see beside her. "I'm still not real comfortable with this. I'm afraid of getting lost in this whole process. I still don't know for sure whom I can trust, and," she paused, twisting her hands nervously, "and, I still don't know if I'm going to buy into all this "God loves me" stuff. I HATE Justin, and I don't think you or anyone else can protect us from him." Elizabeth stood up and started walking away, but stopped and stood with her back to Andrew and Angela. She trembled slightly, and then said in a voice that was barely above a whisper, "I'm not sure any of this is really worth the effort."

Angela and Andrew sat in utter bewilderment as Elizabeth hurried down the hall to her room.

Chapter 13

Sunday was a quiet, uneventful day for the most part. Grace seemed fairly relaxed and spent a lot of time writing in her journal. There was no repeat of the previous day's problem between Elizabeth and Lizzy. The weekend staff was able to report Monday morning that she had played a card game with a couple of the other women and actually sat and watched the Sunday afternoon movie. She seemed to be in a hopeful mood when she went to bed Sunday night, saying she was looking forward to her first real session with Dr. Elgin. She wanted very much for it to go well.

Monday, July 3rd, Andrew again escorted Grace to Dr. Elgin's office right after lunch. This time, Grace didn't lose her lunch. As they walked together down the hall, Grace shyly said, "Andrew, I've never thanked you for saving my life the other night. I want you to know that I am very glad you got to me in time."

Andrew didn't look at Grace. "Hey, no problem, you'd do the same for me."

Grace walked in silence beside him thinking about what he said. Suddenly she started chuckling, visualizing herself trying to support the hunk of a man who walked beside her. Andrew glanced over at her, and then sheepishly grinned. "Yeah, I just got the same picture in my mind."

They stopped just outside Dr. Elgin's door. Grace turned to Andrew and spoke, "Thank you again, Andrew, and thank you for making me feel so safe with you. That's not an easy task, you know."

"It's my pleasure, Mrs. Anderson."

Andrew knocked on the door and Dr. Elgin called for them to come in. Andrew opened the door for Grace. As she walked in, Andrew whispered, "I'll be waiting out here if you need me. Break a leg, kiddo!" he winked at her as he closed the door.

Grace smiled, laughing softly to herself. Dr. Elgin was walking around his desk as Grace looked up and he motioned toward some chairs sitting in front of a huge fireplace. "Let's sit over here. I think we'll be more comfortable."

Grace sat down in one of the large overstuffed leather chairs. They were much more comfortable than the hard straight back chairs in front of the desk.

There was a small tape recorder and several tapes sitting on a table beside the chair where Dr. Elgin was sitting. Dr. Elgin held two files in his hand. Dr. Evans had probably sent one, the rather thick file up, and the thinner file with hers and the hospital name on it, Dr Elgin had probably put together.

Dr. Elgin pulled out a legal pad, and picking up his pen, jotted down the time. He then set the pen down, pushed the record button on the tape recorder, took off his glasses and looked at Grace.

"Grace, before we begin, I want you to know that Angela has recorded a couple sessions that she had with you on the unit. I will also be recording our sessions and there may be times when we will listen to some of them. Let me explain the purpose for this." He paused for a moment, watching closely Grace's reaction to what he was saying.

Grace didn't move. She fought to

144

make herself keep eye contact with Dr. Elgin. Her mind raced. *Stay focused, Grace. You can do it. Slow, deep breaths, just relax. I need to know what is happening and be able to remember what is said.*

Dr. Elgin cleared his throat and continued. "The purpose for recording our sessions is for me to be able to review what was said, and to capture on tape any proof of possible alternate personalities. It will be important for you to be able to "hear" their voices so you can begin to accept them and we can all work together toward helping you become a whole person."

Grace could feel panic welling up inside her. *Please, Jesus, help me.* Suddenly, Grace felt a kind of tingling all over her body and very carefully folded her hands in her lap. So many different emotions seemed to be washing over her. She wanted to answer Dr. Elgin in a clever smart way that she did not need to "hear" proof of the existence of these other personalities; she already knew they were there. *I do?* And, she was well able to control herself and not let her emotions get the better of her. *I can?* But she also felt like jumping up on the chair and yelling that she was tired of always being in trouble when most of the time it wasn't her fault! And why couldn't she go out side more often? And why didn't they have any good movies? *What's going on?*

Grace suddenly realized that Dr. Elgin was talking to her. "I, I'm sorry, what did you just say?"

"I asked if you understood the need for me to tape the sessions." Dr. Elgin looked closely at her.

The pins and needle feeling sent

shivers up and down her spine as she very carefully slid forward to the edge of her seat. "Yes, I guess I do understand the reasoning. What I don't understand is the strange thing that just happened to me."

Dr. Elgin picked up his pen, and began writing as he spoke, "Tell me what strange thing just happened to you."

Grace rubbed her sweating palms on the sides of her slacks, still tingling all over, like she had just touched something that was sending electricity through her taunt body. "I'm not sure I can explain what just happened."

Dr. Elgin sat quietly watching her, waiting for her to continue.

Her deep blue eyes glazed over for just a moment, and then she was standing, walking over to the fireplace. She turned to look at him, frustration and impatience clearly showing in her eyes now flashing blue thunderbolts.

"Oh, for crying out loud, I'll tell you what happened! *She* wants to make a good impression and *I* just want to get on with this. I don't need any proof that I exist." Grace, who had switched to Elizabeth, was standing with her hands on her hips. With an impatient gesture she flung them up in the air. "See, here I am! I am totally in control of myself and I do not let my emotions get the better of me!"

Dr. Elgin set his pen down and looked thoughtfully at Grace. "Is that so? Hum? Am I to believe I am experiencing the privilege of speaking with Elizabeth at the moment? Am I correct?"

Elizabeth's eyes narrowed as she slowly nodded her head. Suddenly her hands were on her hips again and she stomped her right foot in anger. "This

146

is not fair! I know Elizabeth is going to try and blame all of this on me, but it's not my fault. I always get blamed for everything, and that's not fair! I want to have my turn, just cause I'm the youngest doesn't mean I don't have important stuff to say!" Lizzy's lower lip began to tremble and tears filled her eyes.

Dr. Elgin leaned forward in his chair, looking directly at Grace. "Lizzy, I promise I will listen to you. You are very correct in that you have important stuff to say, and I want to hear it. Do you think you could come back over here and sit down?" His kind and gentle response seemed to melt her anger like ice cream left out on a hot summer's day.

She skipped back over to the chair, spun around and sat down with a playful flounce. Almost instantly her posture changed and her voice changed to a more forced controlled manner. "If you patronize her like Andrew and Angela do, she will never grow up. She will always be getting us into trouble."

Dr. Elgin cleared his throat. "I would like to speak to both of you for just a minute, but first, can you tell me if Grace is listening, and is she aware of what is going on right now?"

Dr. Elgin watched as Grace's body seemed to move in a fluid motion of changes. Her frowning face with scrunched eyebrows and narrow eyes, stiff back and folded arms flowed into a pouting lower lip that started to quiver as her now large round eyes threatened to spill over with tears. Suddenly, her hands gripped the sides of the chair and a confused and near panic stance seemed to take over her body. A strong desire to get up and run made her grip on the

chair tighten to the point her knuckles turned white.
"Grace?" Dr. Elgin questioned softly.
Grace was afraid to move or speak. Her eyes slowly focused on Dr. Elgin's face. He was leaning forward in his chair, looking intently at her.
"Yes." Her response was barely audible.
Dr. Elgin was silent for a moment, reading the panic and fear in her eyes. Slowly and carefully he spoke, "Grace, I am going to talk to you and I am also going to talk to Elizabeth and Lizzy. I don't want you to be afraid or alarmed by anything that happens. I think if you could relax just a little, this will go much easier for you. Do you trust me, Grace?"
Grace's tortured eyes began to fill with tears as she slowly nodded her head and tried to relax her grip on the chair.
"Good. Alright, first I want to talk to Elizabeth. I want you to all listen, but I want Elizabeth to answer me. Do you understand me Grace?" Dr. Elgin waited as Grace slowly nodded her head and then sat up strait and folded her hands.
"Elizabeth, you made the statement that you are always in control, but I suspect that at times you cannot deal with things, and choose to simply, "go away" leaving the dealing of the issue to Lizzy or to Grace. I want you to listen to this. . ." While he was speaking Dr. Elgin had stopped the tape recorder and taken the tape out, picked up another tape and put it in. He then pushed the play button.
"Elizabeth doesn't always like me. She gets mad at me when I get mad and break things." ‹mischievous

giggle> "She likes people to think she never gets mad, but she does. She just holds it all in. She's so C-O-N-T-R-O-L-L-E-D! But I know what she does when she's about to pop." <silent pause> "What does she do, Lizzy?" <silent pause, then a whisper> "She hides, too. She just goes away and if I don't come then poor Grace suddenly finds herself in a strange situation. She feels like she's going crazy. She has a lot of strange feelings and she's mad and hurt. She doesn't know what to do or even what's going on. When she can't figure it out she becomes even more upset. Sometimes I can't help her and then she does stuff that she's ashamed of and then she goes away too and I have to try and fix everything." <crying> "Does that seem right, Angela? I mean, I'm only nine and a half, why should I always have to take the blame for everything?"

Dr. Elgin pushed the stop button, removed the tape and put the first tape back in, pushing the record button. He turned to look at Grace. "You know what I think, Elizabeth? I think you are hurting just as much as Grace is. I think you need Grace and Lizzy just as much as they need you. If the three of you will work together, I believe that you will become ONE whole person, with three parts."

Elizabeth's eyes narrowed as she bit her bottom lip, her hands alternated clenching and unclenching.

"Elizabeth, are you familiar with the concept of "the trinity" in the religious world?" Elizabeth's eyes opened wide, and she whispered, "Yes, I know about God the Father, God the Son, Jesus, and God the Holy Ghost."

Dr. Elgin leaned back in his chair and continued, "We humans are a lot like the trinity. We have a body, a soul and a spirit. I also believe that our spirit can have many different parts. One part is better able to cope with serious issues; another part is able to handle humor and less serious issues.

Another part may be able to cope with sorrow and pain, while yet another part may have difficulty handling reality and is better able to function in a make-believe world. Most people are aware of these different aspects of their personality. Sometimes, due to trauma or abuse or maybe a stressful situation, a person's personality can fracture, and then the main personality is usually unaware of the fractured personality." Dr. Elgin paused to smile at Grace. "Have I totally confused you yet, Elizabeth?"

Elizabeth seemed to have relaxed as Dr. Elgin was speaking, and carefully flicked a piece of lint from her sweater. "No, you haven't confused me. But I'll tell you what I think. I think *I* am the main personality, and I am aware of Lizzy and Grace, they are the fractured parts and I think *I* should be in control at all times from now on."

Her body began to shake violently and she suddenly stood up with such force that the heavy leather chair tipped over with a loud thud. The door to the office opened suddenly and Andrew was in the room in an instant. Dr. Elgin held up his hand and Andrew remained at the door. "Lizzy?"

Lizzy stood facing Dr. Elgin, her hands balled up in fists. "I told you!" she screamed, "I told you she hates me. But she also hates Grace. Yes she does! She wants to be rid of both of us. She's so stupid. She's not even listening to you. I'm only nine and a half and I understand that I can't make Grace or Elizabeth leave without making myself leave too." Lizzy was panting for breath as she looked over at Andrew, and tears filled her eyes. "Andrew, I think Elizabeth tried to get rid of

Grace and me when Grace tried to hang us. I don't want to go away! Please make Elizabeth be nice!"

Dr. Elgin nodded at Andrew and he stepped back out in the hall, quietly closing the door behind him. Dr. Elgin set his tablet of paper down and looked at Lizzy. "Lizzy, can you sit back down on the chair and let me talk to Grace?"

Lizzy set the chair back up and sat down, brushing the tears from her eyes. She sat for only a moment and then looked up at Dr. Elgin and said in a trembling voice, "Dr. Elgin, please tell me I'm not insane. I'm trying very hard to understand what you are saying about personalities fracturing. I want to understand. I hope what has happened in here today is not going to make you feel like I cannot get better. I'm scared, Dr. Elgin."

Dr. Elgin inwardly sighed with relief, Grace was back. "Grace, you are definitely NOT insane. I very much believe that you can become a whole person, without losing any of the different aspects of your personality. Elizabeth is going to come around I'm sure, she's just feeling very vulnerable right now. We're going to do some looking back in our next session to see if we can determine just when your personality fractured, what happened to cause it to fracture and help you come to grips with your feelings and the others' feelings about the incident." He stood after turning off the tape recorder. "You don't have to be afraid, Grace, we're going to work through this together, all of us. OK?"

Grace nodded. "Thank you, Dr. Elgin."

"Before I see you next Monday, I would like each of you to take some time to write down anything you can remember, and also how you feel about the things you remember. Do you think you could all do that?" He looked at Grace, waiting to see how she would respond to his request.

Grace stood by the chair, holding it tightly for support. Her eyes became large and glazed. Suddenly, she tipped her head and scuffed one of her shoes against the leg of the chair. "Can I draw a picture? Like a picture story?"

Dr. Elgin smiled, "Yes, Lizzy, you may draw me a picture. That would be wonderful."

Her position changed immediately to arms folded and her back turned to him. Agitation and frustration dripped heavy with sarcasm as Elizabeth replied through clenched teeth, "This is such a waste of time, but I guess if I'm to get a fair evaluation of this whole thing I'll have to do what you request."

Grace's shoulders suddenly slumped and she turned to shakily grab hold of the chair again for support. She raised troubled eyes to look at Dr. Elgin. "I did bring my journals from the last twelve years with me. I've been reading through them and found three different types of handwritings. I highlighted the two I did not recognize and left mine alone. Do you want me to bring them with me next time?"

Dr. Elgin reached out and gently took hold of Grace's arm. "Yes, Grace, that would be very good if you could bring them with you next time." He slowly walked Grace to the door reminding her that she would be seeing one of the students from the university that worked with him on Wednesday and Friday for about an hour each time and that he would see her again the next

Monday. There was no mention of moving her to another unit, for which Grace was really glad, as she did not feel ready to leave Angela yet.

At the door, Grace turned to Dr. Elgin and said, "Thank you again, Dr. Elgin, for all you are trying to do for me. I really do appreciate it. I am trying very hard."

Dr. Elgin had patted her on the shoulder and said, "I know you are, Grace, and you're doing just fine. You all are. This is really going to be OK. Trust me."

Andrew was sitting on the window ledge, again. He looked up at her and smiled. "All ready then?" Grace nodded, smiling. Andrew grinned. "OK, here we go then."

Coming back onto the unit wasn't as traumatic as it had been the week before, but it still took Grace by surprise to see the strange antics put on by most of the patients. Angela could only spare a quick glance and nod when Grace and Andrew came through the unit door. Andrew grinned and winked at Grace as he hurried over to help Angela with a new anorexic patient, Judy, who was cursing and trying to cut herself with a paperclip.

Grace did not move from where she had stopped just inside the day room. She made herself stand still and take slow deep breaths. *This really isn't that scary. I've seen worse things on T.V. Just relax; it's going to be OK.*

Angela glanced again at Grace, and was pleased to see Grace watching the strange drama play itself out, her head tipped slightly to the side. Her obvious slow deep breaths made Angela smile. As she caught Grace's eye, she winked and then turned back to Judy.

The wink was like a healing tonic. Grace's face broke into a big grin, and turning she walked over to the counter and asked Ann Marie if she could have a pen to write in her journal. Ann Marie looked at Grace and asked, "Where's your journal?"

Grace laughed, "Oops. Sorry. I gotta go get it. I'll be right back." And turning she hurried down the hall to her room.

Ann Marie smiled, Lizzy. She got out a pen and several colored markers and had them ready for when "Lizzy" returned to the desk.

Chapter 14

Grace spent the remaining part of the afternoon writing in her journal. At one point, while she was making a drawing, she seemed to get upset and argue with herself, but finally finished and brought the pen and markers back to the desk.

As Ann Marie took the pen and markers, she asked, "May I see what you drew, Grace?"

Grace was hugging the journal to her chest, but after a moment, handed it to Ann Marie, opening it to the page on which she had been working. Ann Marie looked with shocked amazement at the childish, yet very accurate drawing of a young girl on her hands and knees, with a large hand holding an object that was being pushed up inside the girl. The attention to detail was amazing. Ann Marie closed the journal and looking up at Grace could see the blank look on Grace's face.

"Grace?" she said gently, "I think I'll keep your journal up here for you until you want to write in it again. OK?" Grace nodded but didn't move. "Did you need something Grace?"

Grace reached up and scratched under the foam collar. "Yes. May I have a cigarette?"

Ann Marie smiled. "Sure." She walked over to the shelves that held baskets with each of the patient's names on them and pulled out Grace's. She got a cigarette out and put the basket back and handed the cigarette to Grace. Grace waited for her to light it and then went over to the table that Patty and Elizabeth were sitting at to smoke and talk to them.

Ann Marie opened the journal again

and looked closely at the picture. It was amazing the graphic detail that Grace had captured on the paper; the tortured look of fear and pain on the child's face. It was a child's face, and yet it looked old and sad and tired. The hand holding the object was very big, out of proportion to the child's body. It was rough looking; a man's left hand, and had a ring on the ring finger.

The object, Ann Marie squinted hard, trying to make out the detail, looked like a tube, yet it was rounded on one end and had little bumpy knobs all over it. Ann Marie frowned at the multiple red lines drawn from where the object was being inserted into the girl. There was a mixture of lines; some long some short. She counted twenty-five in all. There appeared to be a red puddle under the back half of the girl. It looked like she was kneeling in it and it extended to the area past the hand.

The strangest part of the picture was all the sets of eyes. They were everywhere on the paper, and all of them were looking at the girl and the hand.

Ann Marie closed the journal and then wiped her hands on the sides of her pants. A shudder ran through her; like you get when you feel like someone has just walked over your grave. She would definitely show the journal to Angela as soon as she was free. She looked over at the table where Grace had gone to sit and smoke. Grace was holding some cards in one hand and the cigarette in the other. Suddenly Ann Marie realized that Grace was looking at her. She knew she could not turn away like she wanted to. Their eyes remained locked for a minute, until Grace finally looked back down at her cards. Ann Marie sat down on the stool, propped her elbows on the counter top and lowered her head. *My god, what kind of a horrible sick life did that poor woman have to live through?*

After dinner, Ann Marie gave Grace's journal to Angela. Angela took it into her office and sat down at the desk to read what Grace had written after getting back from her session with Dr. Elgin and to look at the drawing that Ann Marie had been so anxious for her to see. Angela did not realize that she was crying until a wet drop smeared one of the eyes on the page. She quickly blotted the journal with a tissue and then wiped her eyes with a clean one. She felt sick to her stomach. She turned back two pages to read what Grace had written.

Monday, July 3rd, 1989

I had my first "real" session with Dr. Elgin today. I'm not sure that it went very well. I tried to tell him about the mixed emotions I was feeling, the separate emotions, but then Elizabeth's voice ended up talking and then the Lizzy voice, and well they kind of got into it. Oh, it was so confusing and scary. I think maybe some of the feelings were mine and yet it seemed like they were someone else's too. I think I was actually aware of the two different personalities. This is so strange; I'm still not totally convinced that it is all real. It's kind of like being in a movie. Sometimes I get to watch and sometimes I don't. It's very scary. Some of the feelings are so strong, so full of anger and pain. I'm beginning to think that a lot of the really bad dreams I've had all my life are probably buried memories. I wish Mum and Dad were still alive. I miss them so much and really need them.

Suddenly the handwriting changed.

I really like dr elgin, he's really nice to me. He didn't get to ask me very many questions, but he did listen to what I said. He didn't laugh at me neither. He said we're going to try and look back and see what happened to factur us and said I could draw him pictures cause I like to draw, so I'm gonna draw a picture for him. I gonna make a picture about something that happened to me, like a story, and how I feel when stuff is happening to me? Elizabeth had better not get mad at me!

The handwriting changed again for the third time.

I really think this whole thing is going to be a big waste of time. I think it was confusing for Grace, but considering how Lizzy acted, Grace really did well, all things considered. I still think that I really am the main personality, and I should be in control most of the time. I don't see the problem with that. Lizzy needs to chill out or just go away. She thinks Dr. Elgin is going to be interested in her drawings. What ever. I'm going to write out some things for him.

Angela looked up from her reading. It was almost time to hand out the evening medications. She closed the journal and went out to the medication cart. Before getting her clipboard, she put Grace's journal back in her basket.

As Angela handed out the medications, she noticed that Grace was not in the day room, and glancing around, she noticed that all of her staff was. She felt a sudden chill, and catching Andrew's eye, motioned for him to come to her. As Andrew came up to her, she asked quickly, "Where's Grace?"

Andrew looked quickly around the room, glanced at Angela and gave a quick shake of his head, and then turned and hurried down the hall toward Grace's room. *PLEASE GOD*, was his urgent silent petition.

As Andrew approached Grace's door, his stomach tightened in a knot. What

158

was he going to find? Cautiously, he peeked around the corner into the room. Grace was sitting cross-legged on the bed looking at the one photo album that she had brought with her. She looked up just as Andrew poked his head around the corner, and smiled.

Andrew grinned back, a slight flush spreading over his face. "Sorry, we didn't know where you were. Angela's passing out the night meds. What ya lookin' at?"

Grace patted the bed beside her, "Just some pictures I brought with me." Andrew sat down beside her, thankful he could sit since he felt a little weak in the knees.

Pointing at a picture of a small girl standing beside a woman next to an older model car, he asked, "Who's that?"

Grace flushed, "That's my mother and me. I think I was 8 years old in this picture. That would make it 1969. The car is a '68 Olds. It was the first brand new car my parents ever bought. My dad was so proud of that car. They saved for a long time and he was able to sell his old car so he almost paid cash for it."

Andrew looked at the picture. The woman looked to be in her late 30's. She was tall, with the short puffy hairstyle of the 60's. Her eyes looked tired and strained. The little girl, Grace, had a distracted look on her face, very similar to an expression he had seen before on Lizzy's face. Her hair hung in pigtails. She had on a little plaid dress and she was holding a small child's purse. She had on white ankle socks with lace trim and black patent leather shoes with a buckle. Andrew glanced at another picture.

"Who's that?" he asked and pointed

to a tall rustic looking man. He appeared to be standing beside the same car as the one in the last picture. Grace smiled, "That's my dad. He was so big and tall and handsome. He was the best dad in the whole world." Grace's voice caught as she tried not to cry. "Both of my parents were killed in a car accident four years ago this past February 20th. I guess I still really miss them."

Andrew looked at Grace, "Hey, you don't have to apologize for missing your parents. Losing a parent is hard enough without having to feel like you need to apologize for feeling sad that they are gone. Parents are an important part of our lives. They're key figures. To have both of them taken, suddenly, without warning must have been very traumatic for you. It sure would have been for me. It's one thing to lose someone to very old age or to an ongoing illness, but to suddenly lose them because of an accident, wow I sure wouldn't want to have to go through something like that." Andrew turned the page of her album, "I'm sure your husband was a real comfort to you at the time."

Andrew turned another page in the album before he noticed Grace's hold on the book tighten. It was only then he realized she had not answered him. Slowly, he raised his eyes to look at her and was stunned by the kaleidoscope of expressions flowing across her face.

Suddenly, Grace seemed to cave in on herself. Very softly she whispered, "He was very impatient with me. He said I was too old to be acting like such a child." Tears were now running down her cheeks. "He said, "Everyone dies sooner or later. Deal with it." Grace sniffed and quickly rubbed the tears away, "Can you believe that?" she asked, her voice suddenly hard and bitter, "He is such a callous prick!" Grace took the album from Andrew, and closing it, hugged it to her, rocking gently on the bed. "Andrew, can you tell me what a 'prick' is?"

Andrew sat staring, open mouthed at Grace. Suddenly he grinned, and scratching his head, cleared his throat, "Lizzy?" Lizzy turned her head to look at Andrew and nodded. *I thought so!* Andrew stood up and reached for her hand, "Let's go get your night time meds and I'll see if I can try and explain to you what that word means, OK?"

Lizzy smiled, nodding her head, and stood up. She set her album down on the dresser, took Andrew's hand, and walked to the day room.

Angela saw Andrew and Grace come out of her room walking hand in hand, and knew at once that it was Lizzy he was walking with. She watched, with some amusement as Grace suddenly stopped, and putting her hand over her mouth, gave Andrew a shocked look. Then she playfully punched him in the arm as he shrugged his shoulders. Lizzy turned and ran over to Angela.

"Angela, do you know what the word 'prick' means?" Lizzy asked, standing first on one foot, then the other. Angela looked past Lizzy at Andrew. He stood several steps back of Lizzy, both hands in his pockets, and again shrugged his shoulders. "Yes I do, dear. It's kind of a crud word that I would suggest you not use again, OK?"

Lizzy grinned, reaching for her pills and water. "OK." After Angela checked to be sure she had swallowed her pills, Lizzy turned to go back to her room, but stopped when Angela spoke.

"Lizzy, I need to talk to Grace for a while. Will you come with me to my office?" Angela headed back toward the nurses' station door to put the medication cart away.

Lizzy slowly turned and followed Angela to the office. Once inside, she sat down at the table and waited for Angela. When Angela came over to the table and sat down, she had Grace's journal. Lizzy looked at her in alarm, "Am I in trouble?" she asked.

"No Lizzy, you are not in trouble. I would just like to talk to you and Grace about your drawing. Is that OK?" Angela sat with her hands folded on top of the closed journal.

Lizzy chewed her bottom lip for a moment, and then nodded her head.

Angela smiled. "OK. Is there some way that you can let me know that Grace is listening too?"

Lizzy took a deep breath, tipping her head to the side, and said, "I think she can hear if she wants to."

Angela was silent for a moment, collecting her thoughts then she asked, "Lizzy, Ann Marie said she asked to see your drawing, and after she saw it she thought that I should see it. So I looked at it this evening, after dinner. You're really quite a talented artist. Your drawing is so detailed, and full of emotion. Do you mind if we look at it together, and maybe you could tell me a little about it. Most artists, when they create a really emotional drawing, have a story that goes along with it. Do you want to tell me about this drawing, and the story behind it?"

Lizzy was silent, staring at the closed journal under Angela's hands. She finally looked up at Angela. "Am I in trouble for what I drew?"

Angela reached over with one hand and took hold of Lizzy's hand. "Lizzy, you will never be in trouble for expressing your feelings about something, as long as the way you express those feelings do not hurt or offend anyone. Feelings are feelings. There is no "right" or "wrong" feeling. We can't control "how" we are going to feel about any given situation. What we can control is how we "express" those feelings, what we do with them. For example; if someone pulls out in front of me when I am driving and I have to slam on my breaks, or swerve to keep from hitting them, I can guarantee you that I am going to be angry at their irresponsible driving. I may honk my horn at them. Some people may shout a cuss word at them or "flip them off." These are not very nice ways to respond to someone, even when what they did was also wrong. What you can't do is try to run them off the road, or rear-end them on purpose, or drive up beside them and pull out a gun and shoot at them. Do you understand what I am trying to say about handling how you respond to situations and feelings?"

Lizzy was sitting with her elbows on the table with her chin in her hands. Her eyes were large with wonder. She sat up and grinning said, "Ya, Elizabeth has done that "flip them off" thing, and I've heard a few words that I wasn't sure what they meant." Lizzy sat back, pulled her legs up and tucked them under her. "I'm glad I don't have to drive yet. There are too many crazy people out there. Elizabeth is all the time talking to them, which doesn't make sense to me, since they can't hear her.

I guess it makes her feel better. It just makes me laugh!"

Angela chuckled at Lizzy's response, and then opened the journal to the page that held the drawing. "Why don't you tell me about your drawing? I can already feel the emotion, but tell me, in your own words, what you were trying to say with this picture."

Lizzy tensed up as she stared at the picture, her face paled and her hands became sweaty. Suddenly, she reached over and picked up the journal. She swallowed and turned the journal so it was facing Angela, and held it with one hand back against her chest and pointed with her other hand.

"Well, this is a picture of me, of how I feel when "things" are being done to me by other people. This big hand here," and she paused to point at the hand holding the tube, "this hand is Justin's hand. He likes to stick things up inside of me. Lots of times it hurts. That's what all the red is. He doesn't care that it hurts me. It doesn't always hurt me where he's putting it, but it hurts me here, and here." She pointed to her heart and her head.

"The eyes are every one who knows me. They don't really "see" this happening to me, but they know something is not right, but they just "watch", they don't DO anything to help me. I don't think they care. They're afraid of Justin. I'M afraid of Justin. But, I don't cry. See?" She pointed to the one eye on the girl. "See? No tears! If there were, the whole page would be red and black!"

Angela watched Lizzy's face as she asked her next question. "Grace, how do you feel about the picture and what

164

Lizzy said?"

Lizzy's eyes suddenly went very large and her hands began to shake. Very slowly she set the journal down and sat staring at the picture. Slowly, tears began to stream down her cheeks. Angela knew Grace was getting ready to speak. With a voice barely above a whisper she answered. "Why would anyone want to do the things he does to another person? I thought if you loved someone, it was kind and gentle. Oh, I'm not saying there can't be passion, but *THAT* is not passion. It's *EVIL*!! And he enjoys it. It "turns him on." How could I have been so blind? And I am afraid of him, very afraid. But I'm also scared to be alone. I don't have any family left. What am I going to do? Sometimes I feel so lost and alone."

Grace lifted sad, tired eyes to look at Angela, the tears still falling. Suddenly, a soft smile touched her lips. "I keep thinking about that song I heard on the radio the other morning. Something inside of me tells me that it was a "moment from God," just for me. When I first saw the drawing, I was really upset. I think I was upset because there it was, in full color, the horror, the indignity of it all. All the feelings I had been trying not to feel were staring me in the face. Then I thought about the song, and I did again what the guy said to do. I just called out: J E S U S, and suddenly I knew I wasn't really alone. And do you see these eyes up here?" Grace picked up the journal and pointed to some lines that Angela had not really noticed until Grace pointed at them.

"You see the eyes don't you? Do you know whose eyes those are?" Grace's voice shook with emotion, but she was smiling through her tears. "Those eyes belong to Jesus, and *HE* is big enough to handle it for me. So, I'm just going to keep holding on to Him!" Angela didn't realize she was crying until she felt the tear hit her hand. She smiled at Grace, and Grace smiled back.

    God was saving Grace, all by Himself!

Chapter 15

It was not until after dinnertime the following day that Grace realized it was the 4th of July. Angela was not on the unit when she woke that morning. Instead, there was a woman who sometimes was there when she would wake up in the night. Grace was disappointed, but she kept busy reading her Mother's Bible, and playing card games with some of the other women. She was nervous, and found herself "thinking" a silent prayer to Jesus whenever she started feeling the need to pace the floor.

After dinner, they were told that once it was dark they were all going to go outside to see some fireworks. That was when Grace realized that it was the 4th. She was happy they were going to see fireworks, but sad to think she was in a mental hospital viewing them. She felt agitated to think *she* was stuck in here, when really it was *Justin* who was sick!

Grace mentally shook herself, and spoke firmly in her head. *OK, girls, we're going to behave ourselves. We're here, so let's make the best of it. I really feel like we're making headway, so let's not get into any trouble!*

Grace shook herself again and suddenly chuckled out loud. *Well, that's the first time I've ever done that!*

Grace wrote in her journal until Susan and Philip started gathering the women to go outside to watch the fireworks. The air was chilly as Grace sat on one of the benches and hugged her sweater around her for warmth. The fireworks were spectacular and Grace found herself wishing that Pat could have been with her to enjoy them. She did not think about Justin at all.

Wednesday morning Grace was up before Penny came around to wake them. She was dressed and walked to the nurse's station to wait to get her bathroom things to brush her teeth. She knew that one of the University students who worked with Dr. Elgin would be coming to see her and she wanted very much to make a good first impression.

After lunch, Angela came to get her and took her into the office room where they usually had their meetings. A rather young looking woman was sitting at the table and stood up when Grace entered the room. She smiled at Grace and held out her hand.

"Hello, Grace. My name is Kathy. I am a student at the university and I am interning under Dr. Elgin. I'm going to be meeting with you today and we're going to be talking a little about "Why" you are here, and about "What" you would like to accomplish while you are here. OK?" Grace took her outstretched hand and shook it. Kathy was smiling at her. Grace smiled back and sat down in the chair across from Kathy. Kathy looked over at Angela and nodded and Angela slipped out of the room, closing the door behind her.

Kathy opened a thick file in front of her and took out a yellow legal pad, and picking up a pen, she pushed the record button on the tape recorder, looked at Grace and said, "So, tell me, why are you here Grace?"

Grace swallowed hard, and felt herself tensing up inside. *Why do I have to go over all of this again? Don't they know that this is very upsetting for me? Why do I have to keep going over and over and over the same old thing?* Then it was as if she could feel herself relaxing and a new feeling came over her. *Just humor her. Tell her what she wants to hear. The sooner you do that the sooner I can say what we're really feeling and how I'm looking at things differently.* And NO temper tantrums, Lizzy!!

Grace rubbed her forehead for a moment, trying to clear her thoughts and not get upset. She knew what was happening or what she thought was happening. She was arguing with herself, trying to stay calm and do what she had to do and not get upset and lose control, and yet still be able to say what she was really feeling. Was it really three different personalities, or was she just doing what every one did, psyching herself up to deal with something that wasn't pleasant, but still didn't really want to do it and yet knew she had to do it?

This could drive someone crazy all by itself without all the other garbage added to it.

Grace looked at Kathy again, who was calmly waiting for her to speak. Suddenly she remembered. *Jesus! Help me! I can't talk about this by myself! I need to know You are here with me, and going to help me through it.* And suddenly, it was there; a peace and calmness that should not have been there, but was.

"I'm here, Kathy, because I didn't know how to deal with things that happened to me in the past or things that are happening to me right now. I tried to end my life by taking an overdose of my medication. Yes, a lot of really bad things did happen to me and I think I found a way to "forget" them, to pretend that they happened to someone else. I know that sometimes I would just slip away to another place in my mind; a fantasy world, and then after a while, I wasn't able to tell what was real and what was my fantasy. Other times I would just totally lose control. I would say terrible things, swear, and even break things. But I knew losing control was "wrong." I was ashamed of my behavior. How could I act that way? Then I would retreat to my fantasy world, but somehow on the outside, I would still continue to function. Maybe that's called multiple personalities, or maybe it's just me not wanting to be held responsible for what I say and do when everything is just too much to deal with. I'm not real sure about that yet. But I know that from now on I am going to take responsibility for what I say and do, and when it starts to feel too overwhelming, I think what I need to do is remember that Jesus sees and understands the depth of my pain and sorrow and frustration. I know that He will stand with me throughout the entire process that I know I am going to have to go through to heal all the past hurts, all the past "bad" things that happened to me, and to face up to all the past mistakes that I have made."

    Grace paused, smiling at the open-mouthed, astonished look on Kathy's face, and then continued. "I'm starting to realize that in my weakness and inability to cope, I have someone who can and will hold me up and help me through it all. Someone who, when I want to shout and scream and lose control because it's all just too much, will give me a peace and a calm that passes all understanding and comprehension. He will stand with me throughout the entire healing process with an open heart and open arms. There is nothing that I can pull up out of the depths of my agonizing hurts, and raging soul that God has not heard or seen, nothing that He doesn't already know and understand, and He will still receive me with love and grace."

Grace laughed softly; shaking her head as tears suddenly fell. A sweet smile spread across her face as realization hit home. *GRACE!! What was it her daddy had said? The reason they had given her the name "Grace?" What was that scripture verse he had quoted? "Because by grace you have salvation through faith; and that not of yourselves: it is given by God; Not by works, so that no man may take glory to himself. For by His act we were given existence in Christ Jesus to do those good works which God before made ready for us so that we might do them."** Why didn't I see that before?*

Grace looked at Kathy and smiled. "Kathy, I know this isn't going to be easy. I have a lot that needs to be healed in my spirit, and I guess in my mind too. I know the steps I am going to have to take are probably going to be agonizing. I will probably have failures along the way; old habits are hard to break. But now I know that I don't have to try and do it all alone. I have Jesus to help me. That's what's going to keep me moving ahead. Even in the midst of my failures, Jesus will keep right on loving me because of His mercy and grace, and as long as I hold on to Him, I will make it!"

Kathy was still staring at Grace in amazement. Suddenly she blinked, and quickly looked down at her blank yellow pad. She cleared her throat and spoke,

*Ephesians 2:8-10 *The Bible in Basic English*

"Well, Grace, that was quite amazing. I'm very glad I taped this, because I want to play it back again to be sure I understand what you just said." She jotted a quick note, and then looked back at Grace, "So, am I understanding correctly that you are embracing "religion" to get you through any difficulties you will have to face in the future? Are you saying that "religion" is going to help you face all the "bad" things that happened to you in the past, and that you will be able to work through it all and come out of here a "whole" person?"

Grace laughed. "Heavens NO! Trusting in "religion" is probably what helped me to get so messed up in the first place. I'm a "Preacher's Kid!" I was practically raised in "The Church." But that didn't help me to be able to talk about what was happening to me or to be able to cope with my own shortcomings and failures. All it did was show me how very "bad" I was. I was suffocating in all the condemnation I was feeling, because I couldn't live up to what I thought I had to be so that God would love me and answer my prayers. Because I couldn't see the truth, I didn't know how to be all God planned for me to be. I didn't understand that I needed to have a personal relationship with Jesus Christ. I needed to learn what and who He really was. That's the only way I would really understand what repentance, true repentance, really was. Repentance is a change of heart, acknowledgement of MY sin, and turning from it back to God."

Kathy shook her head in confusion. "How is that going to help you to become a "whole" person, so that you don't have to depend on these other personalities to help you function?"

      Grace smiled. "There's a verse in the Bible that says, *"I can do all things through Christ, who strengtheneth me."** That is how I am going to become what you call a "whole" person. No one is whole. No on is truly complete, until they realize their need for Jesus Christ." Grace brushed a tear from her eye. "You know what's so very sad about all of this?" Her voice broke as Kathy slowly shook her head. "I really should have known all of this. I just wasn't listening. I was so scared and ashamed of all that had happened to me, so confused and deceived by all my fantasies that I couldn't see that all I had to do was turn to Jesus and He would help me through all of it. I was angry and rebellious. Yes, it was probably partly because of all that had happened to me, but also, it is our fleshly nature to want to be in control of our self instead of giving the control of our life over to God."

      Kathy sat staring at Grace. Suddenly she realized that Grace had stopped talking. She blushed, wondering how long she had been staring while Grace was waiting patiently for her to say something.

      "I'm sorry; it's just that I guess I wasn't prepared for this kind of a response to my questions. Usually, I get total denial of what has been going on or a full-blown encounter with the other personalities. I'm not sure there's a category for you. You almost sound like you have a handle on this, and probably don't really need to even be here." Kathy paused and suddenly frowned, and turning pushed the stop

*Philippians 4:13 *The Webster Bible Translation*

173

button on the tape recorder. "Drat, I shouldn't have said that on tape." She rewound the tape for a couple of seconds and then pressed play. "…*instead of giving the control of our life over to God."* Then there was silence. Kathy pushed the stop button. She looked at Grace for a second then pushed the record button. "Grace, it sounds like you are ready to really work at getting well, at becoming a *"whole"* person. I'm sure it won't be long until you are ready to go back out in the *"real"* world and live your life to the fullest."

Kathy quickly pushed the stop button before Grace could make a comment, removed the tape from the tape recorder and stuffed the file and tape into her bag and stood up to leave. She looked nervously at Grace for a moment and then smiling said, "Grace, what I just said I truly believe. I think you're going to be just fine and you'll be out of here in no time. I'll see you again on Friday."

Grace turned in her chair to watch Kathy hurry out of the office. *Wow, I guess I really flipped her out with my response.* Suddenly, the door opened and Angela came in. She stood in the door looking at Grace's smiling face. "What did you say to her? She went running out of here like she was being chased by the devil."

Grace grinned. "She wasn't being chased by devil. She was being chased by Jesus." Angela sat down while Grace repeated what she had said to Kathy. By the time she was through, Angela was smiling while wiping tears from her eyes.

"I'll bet that was a first for her." Angela grabbed a tissue, and then turned back to Grace. "Oh, I almost forgot. I heard a song on the radio last night and I went out today for a while and found a tape with the song on it. I wanted you to hear it. I think it will really give you a lift."

Angela went into her office and got the tape and came back into the conference room. She put the tape in the cassette player, pushed play and then sat back down to listen with Grace.

Be not dismayed,
though it seems like the storms will never end.
Be not afraid,
when it seems like you haven't got a friend.
The storms are raging,
but you don't have to run and hide.
The Lord is faithful
to heal the lonely heart inside.
PEACE BE STILL – The Father loves you.
PEACE BE STILL – The Father loves you.
And no matter where you are
or where you've been,
I am sure He wants you to know,
He won't let go.

Be not dismayed,
though it seems like the hurt will never end.
Be still and know
the Father will never let you go.
The pain is raging,
and you don't have to run and hide,
The Lord is faithful,
to heal the hurting heart inside.
PEACE BE STILL - The Father loves you.
PEACE BE STILL - The Father loves you.
And no matter where you are,
or where you've been,
I am sure He wants you to know,
He won't let go.
And no matter where you are,

*or where you've been,
I am sure He wants you to know,
He won't let go. He won't let go.
Jesus won't let go.
He won't let go.**

    Tears were streaming down Grace's face as the song slowly finished. Grace turned and looked at Angela. Angela smiled through her own tears. Grace swallowed hard and then slowly spoke, "Angela, do you really think that God still wants me, even after all the mistakes I've made and the rebellious attitude I've had? Do you really think that it isn't too late for me?"

    Angela smiled at Grace as she carefully put the tape away. "Grace, I truly believe that as long as there is breath in our bodies, it is never too late to reach out and touch Jesus, to give your life to Him. One of my most favorite verses in the Bible is found in 2 Peter 3:9:

    "The Lord is not slack concerning His promise, as some men count slackness; but is longsuffering to us-ward, not willing that any should perish, but that all should come to repentance."**

    "That verse right there tells me God loves me so much that He is willing to wait a lot longer than I ever would consider waiting on someone else. So, in answer to your question: yes. Yes. Yes! Yes! God STILL wants you."

    Angela grinned as Grace suddenly sucked in a deep breath of air as if she had been literally holding her breath while Angela answered her. Angela suddenly pushed the tape across the table to Grace. "Here, I want you to

*Peace Be Still by: Al Denson
**2 Peter 3:9 King James (Authorized) Version

have this. It will be a reminder to you just how much the Father loves you, and that He will never let you go!"

With trembling hands, Grace picked up the tape. With new tears in her eyes, she looked up at Angela as she stood to leave, "Thanks, Angela. Thanks ever so much for helping me, and listening to me, and praying for me."

Angela's heart filled with joy. *Thank you, Father, for the peace You've given me through helping Grace. Bring her even closer to You, Lord, in Jesus name. Amen.*

Chapter 16

Angela knew as soon as Grace came down the hall Thursday morning that she was going to be dealing with Elizabeth. Her brisk walk and clipped response to questions told her something had Elizabeth's tail in a knot.

She watched with growing curiosity as Elizabeth played with her breakfast, finally handing it over to Patty, one of the bulimia patients. Philip had a slight struggle with Patty, convincing her that she did not need the second breakfast, since it would just mean his following her everywhere to be sure she didn't try to "get rid of it" after eating it.

By 11:00 Elizabeth's pacing and periodic slamming down of a book after only moments of looking at it started to get on schizophrenic Madeline's nerves. From one moment of sitting peacefully playing cards, she switched to a wild cat clawing at Elizabeth's back as she walked by the table. It took Andrew, Philip, and Penny to hold Madeline down while Angela got some medication in her.

Elizabeth became hysterical, and Angela finally had to take her into the side office to check out her back to see if she had been injured. Madeline had managed to actually break the skin, even through the T-shirt and sweater. Elizabeth slowly calmed down as Angela cleaned the wounds and put ointment on them.

When she was finished, Angela sat down across from Elizabeth and waited as she blew her nose one last time. Finally she spoke. "Elizabeth, do you want to tell me what has you so upset today?"

Elizabeth sat staring at her hands

on the table. Finally she spoke in a hushed voice, "I don't think that Grace wants my help any more. She doesn't need me. She's getting stronger and I don't know what to do about it. Why should I have to go away just because she's "*got Jesus now*?" What about all the times I helped her? Don't they count for anything?" She pushed the chair back roughly as she stood up and walked around the table to stand by the window that looked out on an enclosed garden.

Angela sat with her hands clasped on the table in front of her, trying to decide how to comfort Elizabeth and reassure her that everything was going to be OK, when suddenly she heard a loud crash. Her head snapped around to see Elizabeth slump forward, her right arm through the window past her elbow, blood spurting like a fountain from numerous cuts. Angela was on her feet and yelling for help just as the door flew opened admitting Andrew. Penny, right behind him stopped and ran back out to get towels.

Together Angela and Andrew freed the now unconscious Elizabeth from the window, blood continuing to spurt in slow motion from the numerous cuts on her arm. Totally ignoring the blood, Andrew lifted Elizabeth and gently laid her onto the table. Slipping his belt off, he looked at Angela, "Tourniquet?"

She nodded her head at him looking over at the door. In frustration she yelled, "We need towels, NOW!" Penny came through the door carrying an armload of towels, with Susan right behind her. They both hurried over to Andrew and Angela to help. Ann Marie came through the door, and after a quick survey of the situation, turned to call

for medical back up from Dr. Abernathy.
 Andrew had the tourniquet applied, stopping the continual spurting of blood. Penny placed towels under Elizabeth's arm while Susan went to get some water to wash off the blood. Angela carefully examined the arm, looking for any pieces of glass. Andrew bent close to Elizabeth's face, still holding the tourniquet tight while talking softly to her.
 Ann Marie came back into the room, followed by Dr. Abernathy and another nurse. Angela stepped back so they could work on Elizabeth's arm. "What happened?" he asked, beginning to clean the wounds with saline solution and gauze pads.
 Angela's face was pale as she looked at the still unconscious Grace. *What had happened?* Her throat felt dry. She turned desperate eyes to Dr. Abernathy and said in a horse whisper, "I don't know. Elizabeth, I mean, Grace, but it was Elizabeth, had been upset about something all day. Then Madeline attacked her and I brought her in here to look at her back to see how badly she had been injured. She was upset, feeling that Grace doesn't want her help any more. I was sitting at the table trying to think what to say to encourage her, and suddenly there was a loud crash, and she had put her arm through the window." Tears were streaming down her face. "This is entirely my fault! I should have been more careful."
 Dr. Abernathy reached to take the suture from the nurse and began stitching. "Don't be ridiculous, Angela, this is not your fault. You cannot predict how these patients will act." He glanced over at her concern

showing in his eyes as she stood clenching and unclenching her hands, tears still streaming down her cheeks. "You are getting too close here, Angela."

Angela shook her head at Dr. Abernathy, chewing her bottom lip, still unaware that she was crying. Dr. Abernathy sighed and turned to look at Andrew. "Loosen the tourniquet a little, Andrew, I want to see where the bleeders are."

It took about eight minutes for him to suture up the two bleeders and to clean and dress the other minor cuts. Once done, he went to the outer office to document Grace's chart. Susan and Penny took the towels to the laundry while Andrew picked up Grace and carried her to her room. Angela went with him and was going to stay with her, but Ann Marie came to tell her Dr. Abernathy wanted to see her before he left the unit.

"Stay with her, Andrew." She whispered and headed for the office, knowing the difficult and sensitive task she had ahead of her. She knew in her heart that Dr. Abernathy was going to tell her he was going to put in his report that Grace should be moved to another unit. Her immediate task was to somehow convince him not to.

Andrew pulled the chair up close to Grace's bed and sat there holding her hand. He felt sick to his stomach. The sight of her slumped against the window, blood spurting from the cuts in her arm, played over and over again in his mind like a bad movie caught in a loop. He would never forget the feeling of panic that had surged through him when he heard Angela scream. Grace seemed to be feeling better, what had happened?

Sudden movements on the bed made him open his eyes and look at Grace. Her deep blue eyes were large with fright. "What happened, Andrew? Why are you here? Why does my arm hurt?"

"Grace?" Andrew questioned, as he looked searchingly into her eyes. Grace bit her lip, and nodded her head.

Andrew heaved a sigh and leaned forward, "Elizabeth was upset, and, well, she put her arm, I mean, your arm through a window in the conference room." He paused for a moment as first shock, and then anger, and finally fear, all flashed across Grace's face. "What's the last thing you remember Grace?"

Confusion now filled Grace's eyes, and she held tightly to Andrew's hand. "I, I remember going to bed. What time is it? Did something happen while I was asleep? I wasn't upset when I went to bed. Why is this happening to me?" Her voice shook with frustration.

Andrew patted her hand. "I'm not real sure, Grace. I do know that Angela talked to Elizabeth before you, I mean, she put her arm, um, I mean your arm through the window." Andrew sighed, shaking his head.

"Andrew?" Grace's voice was soft, yet full of fear, "Andrew, do you think I am crazy? Am I going to be OK?"

"You're NOT crazy, Grace. Trust me. I've SEEN crazy, and that you are not!" he paused for a moment to look deeply into her trusting eyes, and prayed silently that he would never do anything to ever lose that trust. "Do I think you're going to be OK? You bet!"

Angela opened the outer office door and walked through to the conference room where Dr. Abernathy was sitting at the now clean table with

Grace's chart in front of him. He looked up when she entered the room. He could tell by the look on her face he was in for a fight.

He held up his hand when she started to speak. "Wait, Angela, I need to say something before you start in on me. I want you to know that I am only thinking of what I feel is best for you. I think you are getting too close to this case. What happened today was not your fault. I think it would be best for you and maybe for Grace too, if she was moved to another unit. I know you don't agree with me, but I think you should consider it."

"Albert, I knew you were going to say this. I will admit that I was very upset today, but I have not let myself become too close to this case. I truly feel I am not only helping Grace, but I am also helping my self to finally come to terms with Mary Ann's death. When I said it was my fault what happened today, I meant, I knew that Elizabeth was upset and I should not have been quite so lax with her. Albert, you know this is important to me. Please believe me when I say, Grace needs to stay on this unit. I know that I am reaching her and she is really starting to work through this. It's going to take some time, and I am getting the other personalities to start to communicate with her. Grace and the other personalities need to feel safe, and they do here."

Dr. Abernathy sat quietly listening to Angela. Suddenly, the door opened. They both turned to see Andrew standing in the door.

"I'm sorry to interrupt you, but I have someone here who wants to say something to you both." Andrew stepped

184

into the room and Grace followed.

She stood for a moment looking nervously from one to the other. Very quietly she said, "I'm sorry for getting so upset today. I should have just come and talked to you, Angela. I guess I was just scared. I'm trying to understand how Grace could all of a sudden be so able to cope with things. It makes me feel nervous, like I may just disappear. But getting upset and hitting the window didn't really help me, it just hurt me and I'm afraid I've hurt you too, Angela. I didn't mean to cause all this trouble. Please don't give up on us."

"I don't intend to give up on you Elizabeth or Grace or Lizzy for that matter. The three of you are going to work through this, together." Angela turned her head to look at Dr. Abernathy, "I know that God has not given up on you either."

Dr. Abernathy was silent looking from Angela's stubborn face to Grace's hopeful one. He glanced over at Andrew, who grinned and shrugged his shoulders. He sighed knowing he was fighting a losing battle. "OK. You win. I will not recommend she be moved to another unit. This time!" He tore the page from Grace's chart, and started to rewrite his report. "Well, go on, get out of here. I need some peace and quiet to think so I can rewrite this report."

Grace clapped her hands and ran up to Dr. Abernathy and bending down, kissed him on the cheek. "Thank you, thank you, thank you!" She ran back to the door and grabbed Andrew's hand to pull him out of the room after her. Just before the door closed they could hear her say, "That's the first time

185

Elizabeth has ever said she was sorry for anything! I'm not so mad at her now."

Dr. Abernathy raised his hand to touch his cheek where Grace had kissed him. He turned wondering eyes to Angela, who smiled, "Lizzy has a way of really grabbing hold of your heart. Don't say I didn't warn you."

As Angela closed the door, Dr. Abernathy was still sitting with his hand on his cheek. She smiled. *Got ya!*

Chapter 17

After lunch, Angela walked over to the table where Grace was sitting with Andrew working on a puzzle. They seemed to be in a race and were laughing, both reaching for pieces of the puzzle and working fast to find where the pieces went.

Angela pulled up a chair and sat down. "May I watch?" she asked.

Andrew didn't look up, but continued working fast to find where the piece he held in his hand belonged. Grace only paused for a moment to glance at Angela, "Sure."

Angela watched for several minutes as they worked furiously to put the last pieces of the puzzle in place. Laughing, Grace grabbed the last piece before Andrew could and quickly put it in place. With a shout of victory she raised her hands over her head jumping out of her chair and danced a little jig. Andrew flopped back in his chair laughing.

"I won, Angela! I beat Andrew. I'm too fast for him." She giggled with pleasure.

Angela smiled, "Yes, I guess you are." She paused for a moment and then gently asked, "Do you think you could come and talk to me for a few minutes?"

Grace was silent for a moment, searching Angela's face, and then answered, "OK." She looked at Andrew who winked at her and said, "Go on, I'll put the puzzle away. But I want a rematch, and I want a different puzzle!" Grace smiled and then followed Angela out to the day porch.

Once out on the porch, Angela unlocked the outside door and held it open for Grace. "Let's go outside for a

187

walk."
  Grace stepped out into the warm July sun and walked a few steps. She stopped and closing her eyes raised her face to the sky. The warmth of the afternoon sun soaked into her skin like water into a dry sponge. She been outside on Tuesday evening for fireworks, but hadn't been outside during the day since she got the divorce papers. That was last Friday. She had tried to hang herself that evening. Had it really been less than a week since that had all happened?
  Grace opened her eyes at the gentle touch on her arm and turned to follow Angela out into the yard area. There were several picnic tables strategically placed among the numerous flowerbeds, all of which were in full bloom. Their aromatic fragrance was a welcome change from the strong odors associated with the hospital. They sat down at one of the tables close to a flowerbed that was full of activity. Bees buzzed a busy melody as they moved from flower to flower. Every few minutes a hummingbird would dart in to hover over a plant, and then dart away again.
  Grace silently watched the bees and hummingbirds in their busy activity, a sweet calmness washing over her like gentle waves lapping along the shore. She turned slowly to look at Angela as she cleared her throat to speak.
  "Grace, I need to talk to you, but also to Lizzy and Elizabeth." She waited, watching Grace's face for any sign of panic or flight.
  Grace just sat calmly breathing in the different fragrances, so relaxed she felt like she could just float away, high up into the clouds that were

scattered about the sky like large puffs of cotton candy. Slowly her eyes focused on Angela's face. "Wow. I feel so good. Did you give me some new medication with my lunch?"

Angela smiled, "No, just your same meds. But, I have been praying for you since the little incident just before lunch."

Grace's eyes clouded up, "I'm so sorry that happened, Angela. It's so strange; I thought maybe I was past all of that. I guess not yet. Andrew said that Elizabeth is upset. He said she thinks I don't need her anymore and she is afraid that she is just going to disappear. You said that Elizabeth and Lizzy were both just a different part of my personality; parts that I was not aware of or maybe didn't want to be aware of. I thought that I was suppose to be able to start being more aware of my feelings by knowing about them. I thought it was going to be a good thing to be aware of them. How can either of them just disappear? I guess I just don't understand."

Angela took a deep breath, "Grace, I know this is very confusing for you. Before you knew about Elizabeth and Lizzy, they both would function on their own, almost as separate identities. In fact, they did operate that way most of the time. Remember how you said that sometimes you felt strange, like you were watching a movie, or that you were doing something, and yet it did not *feel* like it was you doing it? Then other times, you would just have a large gap in time that you could not account for?"

Grace nodded, listening intently to Angela's words.

"Well, I think that the more aware you become of Elizabeth and Lizzy's emotions and behavior, the fewer times you are going to be "separate" from them. Especially since they are really only feeling the emotions that you are feeling, but do not want to acknowledge for some reason. Their behavior is really your behavior; behavior that either you are ashamed of for some reason or do not want to admit to. As you continue to hold yourself responsible for your feelings and actions, the more in touch with them you will become. So eventually Elizabeth and Lizzy will cease to function *separately* from you. You will eventually always be aware when you respond in your *"Lizzy way"*: young, funny, with almost childlike innocence and trust. You will always know when your more serious, controlled *"Elizabeth"* self responds to situations. You will feel less confused and more complete as Grace with the meshed parts of Elizabeth and Lizzy working with you. Can you understand that?" Angela watched, as Grace seemed to strain to take in everything she had just said.

"Grace, I think Elizabeth is afraid of the change that is going to take place. It won't be the same for her. She will now always just be a part of you, not an identity unto herself. I think that's what she is afraid of. Can you understand that?" She waited, as Grace seemed to struggle with the concept.

Suddenly Grace raised her head to look directly at Angela. "I am afraid of that, Angela. I'm afraid of never again being in complete control of myself. Now, I will always have Grace and Lizzy right there too. What if I want to be alone, if I don't want them with me? What then?"

Angela watched as a small ant slowly worked its way across the table, pulling a very large breadcrumb with its tiny pinchers. Suddenly several more ants came from the direction that the single ant was heading. Soon all of them had a grip on the large breadcrumb and were pulling together. It only took a few seconds for them to reach the end of the table and go over the side and down the leg to the ground. She smiled and looked up at Grace to see her watching the ants also.

"Do you really want to be a lone ant, Elizabeth?" she asked softly.

Grace leaned over the edge of the table to look at the ants moving through the grass. "I don't, Angela! I get to do lots more when I'm part of the whole group." Grace looked back at Angela, her face radiating her Lizzy smile, her eyes full of mischief. Angela laughed softly reaching out to gently touch Grace's cheek with her hand. How she loved this childlike nature of Grace. She hoped that the Lizzy part of Grace would always remain strong in Grace.

Grace's eyes took on a somber look, almost pleading. "Angela, I don't want to be alone, I just don't want to get lost in the whole. Can you understand that? Will I still be me?"

Before Angela had a chance to respond, Grace stood up and reached into her side pocket and pulled out a small New Testament. She sat back down and looked at Angela and smiled. "Andrew gave me this little New Testament during lunch. My mother's Bible is kind of fragile and I don't want to be carrying it around with me all the time. So he gave me this until I can get another complete Bible of my own."

Angela was silent as Grace flipped

through the pages looking for a passage she apparently wanted to read. Who was this, Grace, Elizabeth, or Lizzy?

Grace stopped, having found what she was looking for and looked up at Angela. "You know, Angela, I practically grew up in the church. Do you know that at one time I could quote from memory over 300 Bible verses? Amazing, huh? All that head knowledge and no real heart connection." Her voice broke for a second and then she continued. "There is a passage of scripture in first Corinthians that always confused me, but I think I understand it now. . . ."

For the body is not one member, but many. If the foot would say, "Because I'm not the hand, I'm not part of the body," it is not therefore not part of the body.

If the ear would say, "Because I'm not the eye, I'm not part of the body," it's not therefore not part of the body.

If the whole body were an eye, where would the hearing be? If the whole were hearing, where would the smelling be?

But now God has set the members, each one of them, in the body, just as He desired.

If they were all one member, where would the body be?

But now they are many members, but one body.

The eye can't tell the hand, "I have no need for you," or again the head to the feet, "I have no need for you."

No, much rather, those members of the body which seem to be weaker are necessary.*

Grace's voice was strong and clear as she finished reading. She sat for a minute just looking at the little New Testament in her hands. Finally, she lifted misty eyes gazing past Angela.

"Elizabeth, I know you are listening, and I know you're scared and think I don't want or need you any more, but I do. I can't be a whole person without your wonderful sense of purpose, your strong convictions and stubborn

*I Corinthians 12:14-22 World English Bible

will for right and justice. I always wanted to be able to stand up for myself, but I never could. So you did it for me. What would I have done without you? Now, now I can do it with you. It's going to be so much better now. We can help each other. I don't want to lose any more time. I don't want to be afraid to be, feel, say, all the things that are boiling around inside of me. And if we mess up, well, it wasn't too hard to apologize this morning, was it?"

Angela stared open-mouthed at Grace as she suddenly realized that it was *Grace* who was talking and she was talking to *Elizabeth*! Tears started falling down Grace's cheeks, and she whispered softly, "OK, Grace, we can become a whole person. I'll be strong for you, and Lizzy can keep us young at heart, and you can finally start really living and not feel like you're in a daze all the time. Your sweet gentle nature that is so giving and unselfish will be helpful to me, as I am kind of impatient. We'll complete each other."

Suddenly Grace was on her feet, spinning and jumping and laughing. She did a cartwheel and then rolled around on the grass finally coming to a stop, lying on her back looking up at the clouds, laughing and trying to catch her breath all at the same time. Angela stood up and hurried over to Grace. As she reached her, Grace sat up, the joy of a soul released from a dark prison in her voice, "We're becoming whole Angela, we're becoming whole person!"

Chapter 18

Friday morning, July 7th, Dr Evans came to the hospital for her first visit with Grace. Angela let them go outside to the back fenced yard area so they could have some privacy, and so Grace could enjoy the balmy July weather.

Once outside, they walked over to one of the picnic tables that were positioned under the giant oak trees, and sat down, across from each other.

Grace had been feeling nervous about this first meeting after the fiasco court committal hearing two weeks earlier, but she reached inside herself to feel Elizabeth's strong support and knew everything would be OK. She desperately wanted to be able to share with Dr. Evans all that had been happening. The feeling of tenseness slowly drained from her body and she began to relax, sitting with her hands resting on the table, gazing at one of the huge oak trees several feet away. Without realizing what she was doing, her body began to gently sway back and forth to the same rhythm of the tree branches in the breeze, her breathing slow and deep.

Dr. Evans watched with interest as Grace visibly relaxed before her eyes. She felt a slight twinge of frustration, as she had been hoping to see a manifestation of one or more of the multiple personalities. She set the file holding all the information concerning Grace's stay and the small tape recorder on the table and quickly scanned the notes that had been written by Kathy from her visit on Wednesday. Clearing her throat, she pushed the record button on the tape recorder and spoke to Grace.

"Grace? How are you feeling today? I'm sorry I haven't been up to see you before now, but Dr. Elgin has a very strict 14 day waiting period for visitation, and to be perfectly frank, I'm surprised I was allowed to see you today, after what happened last weekend."

Grace turned to look at Dr. Evans. *I think she's trying to get a rise out of me! I promised I'd be good, and I will!* Grace closed her eyes for a second. *Help me Jesus. Help me to be what you want me to be.*

Grace opened her eyes and looking up at Dr. Evans and smiled. "Well, I'm actually feeling pretty good, Dr. Evans, all things considered. I am very glad you were able to come today. It's important to me for you to know that I'm not mad at you, and I don't blame you for what happened to me on the way here two weeks ago. If anyone is at fault, it's Justin. He knows the law, and would have known the possibilities of what could happen to me while being transported under a court committal."

Dr. Evans eyes became large in amazement. Was this one of the alternate personalities? She glanced down at the file trying to quickly scan the notes to see if it mentioned anything about what happened to her on the way to the hospital. Her head jerked up at the next question from Grace.

"Dr. Evans, did you know that Justin was going to file for divorce? Did he say anything to you?" Grace watched as Dr. Evans fumbled with the file, dropping her pen. Grace reached for one of the bottles of water that they had brought outside with them, and

196

opening it, took a deep drink. "You do know that the whole little act he put on in that poor excuse of a commitment hearing was all just that, an act? I honestly believe it was his plan all along, just in case I failed to really commit suicide." Dr. Evans was now staring open-mouthed at Grace.

Why am I saying all this? Because you're mad, that's why! I thought we were going to be good? Jesus, please help me.

Grace's hand trembled as she quickly took another drink. Dr. Evans still seemed unable to speak.

"Look, I'm sorry I spouted off like that. I guess I'm still frustrated by everything that has happened. I'm trying real hard to be responsible for what I say and do. I want you to know that I'm beginning to understand some things about myself; like the fact that I've always had a problem dealing with things that are too overwhelming for me. I know that I have escaped a lot of times to a fantasy world, when the "real" world was just too much. Sometimes I've been vaguely aware of what I do to cope and other times I guess I just "checked out" and kept functioning on autopilot. Maybe that is what having a multiple personality is, or maybe it was just me not wanting to face up to life and how I was able to deal with everything. I just don't know. But what I do know for sure is that I am choosing now to be responsible for everything I say and do from this point on. Good and not so good. These other parts of me, I am going to use all of them on a conscious level from now on to be a whole person."

Grace paused to see how Dr. Evans was taking what she was saying. She

197

still seemed unable to speak, so Grace hurried on.

"I don't know why all the bad things that happened to me happened. I don't even care any more. I don't want to point a finger and say, "It's your fault!" and I don't even want to go back and make someone "pay." I do know because of all the things I went through, I think I might have a deeper compassion for others who may have gone through similar experiences. I think what I have to offer to people who can't face these things alone is just this: you don't have to face it alone!"

Grace paused again, looking at Dr. Evans as she ran her fingers through her hair while flipping the pages of Grace's file back several pages in an attempt to see if there were any notes to explain the sudden change in Grace. Something must have happened or this was one of the alternate personalities taking over. She looked back up at Grace in frustration.

Grace smiled, and reaching for the other bottle of water, handed it to her. "Dr. Evans, you don't have to worry. It's just me. Yea, I have a lot of mixed feelings right now. Part of me wants to kick and scream how unfair it all is, and another part wants to get in your face for even unknowingly being a pawn in Justin's plan, and another part wants to tell you how I know for the first time that I am not alone. And no matter how many mistakes I make, no matter how many times I fall flat on my face, someone loves me so much that He is only a prayer away."

"You got RELIGION?" The question exploded from Dr. Evans.

Grace grinned. "No, Dr. Evans, I just finally came back to Jesus."

For the next forty-five minutes Grace sat quietly at the table while Dr. Evans read through her chart. Every now and then she would mutter something to herself and flip back a page or two to reread a section and then she would shake her head and go back to where she had been before. Several times she asked Grace a specific question about something she was reading and Grace would try to explain what had happened. In the end, she just sat looking at Grace, trying to sort out all that she had read and trying to make it fit in her psychological mind.

Grace finally glanced at her watch and said, "I think our time is almost up Dr. Evans. They're going to be bringing us lunch soon and then I have my appointment with Kathy again."

Dr. Evans closed the file and slowly stood to her feet. She stood for a moment just looking at Grace. Finally, shaking her head, she held out her hand to Grace. Somewhat confused, Grace reached out and took her hand.

"Grace, I'm not sure I really understand what has happened to you, but I have to say you seem to be coping quite well. I don't know if this is another personality, or if you've had some amazing "religious" experience. Whatever it is, I hope it sticks and continues to work for you. I'll be very interested to read Dr. Elgin's final report."

Dr. Evans picked up the file and tape recorder and they walked back to the building together. At the door, Dr. Evans looked at Grace. "Grace, I'm still going to plan on coming and seeing you at least once every two weeks if that's alright with you. I want to hear how you are doing and also, I want to continue to help you in any way I can."

Grace opened the door and held it for Dr. Evans. "It's alright with me if you want to come and see me, Dr. Evans. I'll be glad for you to see how I'm doing, I'm sure we'll find lots of things to talk about."

Dr. Evans smiled, "Yes, Grace, I'm sure we will. I hope your meeting with Kathy goes well. I'll see you again in two weeks."

Lunch was being served so Grace went to join the other girls while Dr. Evans turned in Grace's chart to Angela and was escorted off the unit.

Grace's meeting with Kathy after lunch was uneventful, in that Kathy was disappointed that she couldn't seem to get either of the two known alternate personalities to identify themselves and talk to her. In the end, Grace felt sorry for her, as she seemed very frustrated that Grace seemed to not need to "switch" as she called it, to either "Elizabeth" or "Lizzy". She could not seem to get it across to Kathy that they were all three talking to her.

The next two weeks went by quickly. Grace was able to slip into a comfortable routine of her appointment on Mondays with Dr. Elgin, and subsequent appointments on Wednesdays and Fridays with Kathy. In between, she had many talks with Angela, did a lot of reading and wrote daily in her journal.

On Tuesday, the 11th of July, in the late afternoon, Pat came up to see Grace. They were taken to a visiting room off the unit, and for the first few minutes Grace clung to Pat, crying.

They visited for almost an hour, with Grace bringing Pat up to date on all that had been happening to her. Pat had brought Grace's mail and they went through it together, with Grace signing checks and making notes for Pat to follow up on the next day. They talked about the lawyer that Pat had retained for Grace, and when the first appointment would be. Pat reassured her nothing was going to happen until she was released from the hospital.

Pat left with the promise of coming back the next week, and Grace spent the remainder of the evening writing in her journal and writing a letter to the attorney.

On Friday, July 21st Grace and Angela waited in the empty unit for Dr. Evans to come for her second visit with Grace. All the other women had been taken outside for some fresh air and exercise. Grace was sitting at the piano, playing a song she had heard on the radio and had written down the words, changing them just a little to fit her own life.

She'd been doing a lot of thinking the last few days. Thinking about how she had ended up where she was. About all that had happened to bring her to where she was. She knew she was tired of disappointing God. Tired of the vicious circle of actions and choices that seemed to trap her in a never-ending pattern of trying to do what she wanted. What she thought was best for her but always falling short. She was tired of not trusting God completely with her life.

Just that morning she had opened her Bible to a verse she couldn't remember ever reading before. It practically leaped off the page at her.

"For I know the plans I have for you," declares the Lord, "Plans to prosper you and not to harm you, plans to give you hope and a future. Then you

will call upon me and come and pray to me, and I will listen to you. You will seek me and find me when you seek me with all your heart."*

That was when Grace's will was finally broken. She read the verse over and over, letting God slowly burn the truth and understanding of it into her heart. Regret and shame threatened to overwhelm her, but that was when God took her into His loving arms and filled her with the quiet assurance that He had never lost track of her. He loved her, just the way she was.

Grace knew she had a problem with forgiving herself. She was also beginning to realize that to forgive herself she had to be able to first forgive others. To be forgiven, you had to forgive. More than anything she was beginning to see the importance in forgiving the people who had hurt her, so that she could finally forgive herself, thus freeing her from one of Satan's most entangling snares. If he can keep people entangled in the web of guilt and shame, they will never be able to move on to all that God has for them.

The most important thing to understand about forgiving others is that forgiving someone else does not change them. Forgiving others changes us. It frees us from the past and from the need to try to seek revenge. Holding on to hidden hate and anger not only affects us, but sooner or later, it will affect any other relationship we may try to have. An unforgiving spirit eventually produces a very bitter person. Bitterness will spill over into our relationships, even with someone we love. In the end, bitterness, not the pain and hurt of the past, is what will destroy us.

*Jeremiah 29:11-13 NIV Translation

Grace knew this to be true, for it had almost destroyed her.

Each day, as she let go of a little bit more of her past, giving it to Jesus, she was finding she was able to forgive those responsible for the wounds, the evil things that had been done to her. And, by forgiving them, she was able to really forgive herself for all the things she had done out of that pain and hurt. With that forgiveness, she tasted for the first time freedom from all the buried hurt and pain; from a broken life and broken promises.

Oh, it was going to take a while for God to restore her to complete wholeness. She knew she was going to still make mistakes. But she also knew that the more she focused on Jesus and the fact that He had a "better plan" for her, the more she would lean on Him and trust in Him. And if she ever found herself thinking she "knew better" than her Lord, well, she knew He would gently rebuke her, and she would feel His love pulling her back and then she would turn and run to Him!

Each new day she was realizing more and more that the God of hope and mercy was really in the business of taking broken people and putting them back together again. Better than they were to begin with. She was also beginning to see that more than almost anything else God loves to take broken, flawed vessels and make them new. Then He uses them for His glory and honor.

The bottom line was she had a choice. She could mire around in the past, in all the pain and hurt, and listen to the enemy of her soul. After all, that was the real battle going on, the battle for her eternal soul. Being deceived, tricked into believing all his lies. Or, she could let the joy of the Lord be her strength. She could give all her hurts to Him. She could give up her right to have someone pay for all the bad things that had happened to her. She could forgive, let go, and forget. She knew deep in her heart, who would benefit most from that choice. Knew who would be totally healed. She would. She also knew that she had to truly desire that healing. She had to truly repent, which meant she had to have a change of heart. She had to desire a relationship with Jesus above everything else.

If you really think about it, if you step back and look at the big picture, instead of focusing on one tiny little part, you will see that in the scope of eternity, our relationship with Jesus is all that really matters. The choice, the decision is ours and ours alone to make. She was making that choice - it was there within her grasp. She was going to begin again!

Her God was the God of new beginnings, of second chances, and sometimes third and fourth chances, and many more than that.

Grace's natural talent and musical training was a joy to see and hear. Angela sat at the counter in a pretense of working on some charts, but she was really listening to Grace.

Grace had borrowed the tape recorder and had recorded a song she had heard on the radio; I Can Begin Again*. She had listened to the song over and over, changing some of the words and then had taught herself to play it by ear on the

*I Can Begin Again, words and music by Larnelle Harris and Dave Clark

piano.

As her fingers ran across the keys, Grace was lost in the music and words and for a moment, forgetting where she was. As she played through the song, she did not see or hear Angela slip out of the office and open the door to the unit, admitting Dr. Evans. Both women walked quietly into the main room and silently sat down to listen to Grace play and sing.

As her fingers played across the keyboard, she ended the chording for an introduction to the song, and then in a clear, pure, soprano voice she began to sing:

"Alone again, in a crowded room,
haunted by the questions in my mind.
It's so hard to understand,
how the life that I had planned,
stole my joy and left me far behind

Though all I had, is lost it seems,
from the shadow of a life that used to be.
I can look beyond the skies,
deep into my Father's eyes,
and see that there is hope in Christ for me.
~
I can begin again,
with the faith of a little child,
my heart has caught a vision,
of a life that's still worthwhile.
I can reach out again,
far beyond the hurt and pain,
with Your arms around me Jesus,
life will never be the same,
for new beginnings are not just for the young.
~
I face the dawn, of each brand new day,
free from all the doubt that gripped my past.
For I've found in trusting Him,

> *every day life starts again,*
> *as I work toward the things that really last.*
> ~
> *I can begin again, with the faith of a little child,*
> *for my heart has caught a vision*
> *that my life is still worthwhile.*
> *And I can reach out again,*
> *far beyond my hurt and pain,*
> *with Your arms around me Jesus,*
> *my life will never be the same,*
> *for new beginnings are not just for the young.*
> *New beginnings are not just for the young.*
> *No, new beginnings are not just for. . . . the young."**

*words changed slightly from original song - see original lyrics in appendix *

As the last chords died out, Grace was startled by the sound of clapping. She turned on the piano bench to see both Angela and Dr. Evans getting up from one of the couches, clapping. Both were smiling and had tears in their eyes. Grace blushed, but then smiled back at them.

Grace stood up taking the paper off the piano on which she had written the words of the song. Angela stepped up to her, and smiling gave her a big hug, whispering in her ear, "That was beautiful, Grace! I just know that God is really going to use you to reach the hurting and broken-hearted out there."

Grace's love-starved heart and soul soaked up the hug and encouraging words like a dry sponge. Tears came to her eyes as she whispered back, "Do you really think so?"

Angela held her out at arms length, looking her straight in the eye. "I don't just think so honey, I know it in my heart. I truly believe that the bad things that happen to us, the things that Satan would love to see destroy us,

God takes those things and turns them around so that the end result is for our good. And the testimony of our lives brings glory and honor to Him!"

Grace longed to believe that all the bad things that had happened to her were not just "bad luck" or "being in the wrong place at the wrong time." Her eyes searched Angela's face for any sign of doubt. "Do you really think so?" she asked.

Angela was so excited she could hardly contain herself. "Grace! Think about it! Think about how Pat started praying for you, right at the exact time that you were attempting to hang yourself! That's not a coincidence! That was Jesus intervening on your behalf. Or think about this. If you had come here two weeks earlier, I wouldn't have been here. I believe that God allowed you to come at this time so I could be here to help you, and ultimately, so you could help me." Tears were streaming down her cheeks.

Grace was puzzled. "I helped you? How?"

Angela stood for a moment trying to regain her composure. Both she and Grace had totally forgotten all about Dr. Evans. Slowly Angela answered, "I had a daughter, Mary Ann. She was a couple of years younger than you. She had MPD. She committed suicide right in front of me just a little over two months ago." Angela's voice broke. Grace stood silently staring at her. "I couldn't reach her. I tried everything I could think of. I loved her so much, but I couldn't help her." Angela's eyes begged for Grace's understanding. "I came back to the unit two days before you came. After I read your chart and started working with you, I just knew

God had sent you here for me to help you find the truth, and by helping you, to heal my own broken heart. So you see, I know God is using you and your life, because my life is one that has already been touched."

Grace suddenly remembered Dr. Evans. She turned to look at her and was surprised to see tears streaming down her face.

Dr. Evans quickly brushed at the tears and smiled. "I'm the second life you've touched. I've allowed psychology to push the God of my childhood right out of my life. Well, not any more. Not any more!"

Grace looked from Angela to Dr. Evans, and suddenly she knew, she was going to be all right. God was taking her broken, shattered life, and was putting the pieces back together for her to begin again. Suddenly grinning, she laughed, clapping her hands. And what a wonderful new beginning it was turning out to be. She knew that from this moment on, her life was going to be anything but dull and broken. She could hardly wait!

Chapter 19

Grace twisted her wedding band and diamond round and round as she waited for the minister of one of the local church's to finish his introduction. She always got nervous waiting for the introduction. She still found it hard to believe that people would come to hear her testimony and sing. She glanced over at Andrew who was sitting just off to her right with their ten-year-old son David and their eight-year-old daughter Pattie. He smiled, giving her their special wink.

She could still remember the first time he had winked at her. He had just walked her to her appointment to meet with Dr. Elgin and had said, "I'll be waiting out here if you need me. Break a leg, kiddo!"

He'd been *"waiting out here"* for the last eleven years. A strong, loving, unexpected gift from God! Grace still trembled with amazement at how awesome God was to bring them together.

Grace had ended up staying the full ninety days at the State Hospital. But it had been a time of healing and growth for her. At the end of her commitment, she had returned to her hometown to struggle through a long and trying divorce. But she wasn't alone. God in His mercy and love surrounded her with friends and professional people who were a tremendous source of strength and encouragement to her.

But her greatest strength came from her continual growing relationship with the Lord Jesus Christ. When the divorce was finally over, Grace moved to upstate Washington. She took some classes so she could do some counseling.

Andrew continued working at the state hospital, but also spent as much time as he could with Grace. They both started going to the small *"House Church"* that met at Angela's every Sunday afternoon.

It was only two years after Grace had met Andrew at the state hospital that they were married in a small service in one of the beautiful gardens on the college campus. Pat and Angela had both cried buckets, causing Grace to laugh with joy as they mopped mascara off their faces, so they could have their picture taken with her and Andrew.

The last eleven years had turned into a ride Grace had never imagined in her wildest dreams of ever having. She had the love and support of a wonderful husband, two very beautiful, healthy children, a comfortable, rustic home in the country, more friends than she had ever dreamed of having, but most of all, she was doing something that she knew the Lord wanted her to do.

She was sharing her story and singing the praises of the One who had pulled her from the depths of her sin, who had taken her lost and hopeless existence and turned it into a life full of His love and glory. Each time she spoke, every time she sang, she was humbled by how God could use the story of her tortured and battered life to bring hope and peace to other lost souls, crying out for someone to show them the way.

Lost in her memories, Grace suddenly laughed softly, shaking her head. God was so amazing. He really had stood with her through the entire healing process. But what was even more awesome was the fact that He had always been there even when she chose not to see Him. He was always there, just waiting for her to open her eyes and look at Him. No, no matter how hard she had tried, she could not hide from Him. He always knew right where she was.

Grace suddenly heard the minister say, ". . . and now, if you will help me welcome her, Grace Burton!"

Grace took a deep breath, *OK, Lord, here we go.*

Grace walked out to the center of the platform, and shook the minister's hand and then turned slowly to look out over the audience. The lights dimmed as the clapping stopped. As she looked over the sea of faces that looked expectantly up at her, she held her breath for a moment. *Let them see only You, Lord Jesus, not me!*

As the music began, Grace closed her eyes and taking a deep breath, began to sing:

You have looked into my heart;
You know everything about me,
You see my deepest thoughts,
and every corner of my soul.
Each single step I take,
and all my words before I speak them,
every place that I have been,
and every place that I will go.
~
I cannot hide from you;
You know me all too well.
There's no story of my life
that Your memory could not tell.
I can ride the morning wings
'til I'm completely out of view.
But, whether in dark or light,
I cannot hide from You.
~
Long before I drew first breath,
You already knew my secrets.
You watched as I was formed,

out of sight from human eyes.
Your Spirit is with me,
and I am always in Your presence.
When I sit and when I stand,
when I sleep and when I rise.
~
I cannot hide from you;
You know me all too well.
There's no story of my life
that Your memory could not tell.
I can ride the morning wings
'til I'm completely out of view.
But, whether in dark or light,
I cannot hide from You.
~
Turn my heart from wicked ways.
Search the whispers of my mind.
And lead me on the road
that will take me home
to everlasting life!

Grace's voice rose to a crescendo, as her arms lifted in worship to her God.

I CAN NOT hide from you; You know me all too well.
There's not a story of my life
that Your memory could not tell.
I can ride the morning wings
'til I'm completely out of view.
But, whether in dark or light, every moment of my life,
I cannot hide . . . . . from You.*

As the music slowly faded, Grace grasped the microphone to steady her trembling body and glanced off stage to where Andrew stood. She could see the tears in his eyes. It happened every time. How could it not?

She was living, breathing proof of God's amazing "Saving Grace"!

~ The End ~

*I Cannot Hide From You: Words and music by: Steve Siler, Scott Krippayne and Tony Wood

Appendix:
*I Can Begin Again
words and music by Larnelle Harris and Dave Clark

Alone again, in a crowded room
Cornered by the questions in my mind
It's so hard to understand
How the life that I had planned
Stole my joy and left me far behind.
Though all I have is lost it seems
From the shadow of a dream that used to be
I can look beyond the skies
Deep into the Father's eyes
And see that there is hope for one like me.
Chorus:
I can begin again
With that passion of a child
My heart has caught a vision
Of a life that's still worthwhile
I can reach out again
Far beyond what I have done
Like a dreamer who's awakened
To a life that's yet to come
For new beginnings are not just for the young.
I face the dawn
Of each brand new day
Free from all the doubt that gripped my past
For I've found in trusting him
That everyday life starts again
As I look toward the things of life that last.
(Repeat chorus twice)
Starting all over again
Is not just for the young
No matter what you've been told
It's not just for the young
It's not just for the young.

Copyright © 1988 Life Song Music Press/BMI/1st Row Music/BMI/John T. Benson Publishing Co./ASAP. All rights reserved. All rights controlled by The Benson Co., Nashville, TN